Glass Slippers Give You Blisters

Mary Jane Auch

AN
APPLE
PAPERBACK

SCHOLASTIC INC.
New York Toronto London Auckland Sydney

ISBN 0-590-43501-9

12 11 10 9 8 7   1 2 3 4 5/9

Printed in the U.S.A.   40

First Scholastic printing, September 1990

For MARGERY CUYLER, who makes writing
(and rewriting) a pleasure!

Glass Slippers Give You Blisters

CHAPTER 1

"Gram! We're over here," I yelled, as I saw my grandparents climb out of their pickup truck in the parking lot.

Mom pulled a foil-wrapped dish from her picnic basket and arranged it with the others on the table. "It's about time they got here. We'll barely have time to eat before the orchestra concert."

"Relax, Mom," I said. "It's Labor Day. You know . . . a national holiday?"

Dad looked up from the newspaper he was reading. "That's right, Ruth. If they catch you not relaxing today, you could get up to thirty days in a federal penitentiary."

Mom has just finished putting little clips on the corner of the tablecloth to hold it down, even though there wasn't any wind. "Relax! You just don't understand how long it takes to prepare a picnic meal. I've been up since six this morning chopping, mixing, baking..."

Gram thunked a brown paper grocery bag on one end of the table, scattering Mom's artistic arrangement of plastic knives, forks, and spoons.

Mom looked up from frosting her Double Dutch Chocolate cake. "Honestly, Mother, the whole town shows up for the Labor Day picnic. Couldn't you have found something decent to wear?"

Gram held out her arms and looked down at her paint-spattered jeans and "Save the Possum" T-shirt with a tire tread running across the chest. "Looks like everything's covered up that ought to be, Ruth. I do have a hole in one of my sneakers, but exposing a toe here and there is no crime, is it?"

Mom was busy lining up forks. "You're impossible." Neatness counts with Mom. It not only counts, it adds, subtracts, and multiplies.

Gram winked at me, then grabbed me in a big hug, rocking me back and forth. "How's it going, Kelly? All set for the big day tomorrow?"

"I guess so. I'm not sure I'm ready for the middle school, though. We never even got to be big shot sixth-graders in the elementary school, and now we'll be the baby sixth-graders in the middle school. It's not fair."

Gram stepped back and looked at me. "You're right. It's a shame that they've switched the grades just when it was going to be your chance to shine."

"Now we won't be the oldest kids in school until ninth grade. That's forever!"

Gram snitched a finger of chocolate frosting when Mom wasn't looking. "Time goes by a lot faster than you think, Kelly. I can't believe you got so old so fast. Kids have a way of growing up when you're not looking, I guess."

Mom cleared her throat and shot Gram a look. "Mother, would you please get your things ready so we can begin? I made some hors d'oeuvres, but now I'm not sure we have time for them."

Gram dug into her bag. "We'll make time for them. I made some hors d'oeuvres myself. Here, Kelly, catch." She tossed me a bag of Fritos and opened a plastic tub of store-bought dip. "This is hot stuff. Jalapeño peppers. It'll knock that rug right off your head, Norm." She gave my father's curly hair a gentle tug, and he laughed. She was always teasing him about his hair being fake, but it wasn't.

Mom shielded her eyes against the bright setting sun as she scanned the park. "What's happened to Father? I thought he was with you when you got out of the truck."

Gram shrugged. "He's probably hooked up with some of his friends. I swear he's getting gossipy as an old woman, in spite of the fact he can't hear a blasted thing."

Mom made one of her sharp little sighs. "Well, we can't start without him."

Gram climbed nimbly over the bench and sat down. "Nonsense. If the man's hungry, he'll find food. Let's see those hors d'oeuvres you were talking about."

Mom pulled the foil covering off a platter of little grayish-brown things and passed them to Gram.

Gram looked closely at the tray and smiled. "Well, aren't those the sweetest little things? Looks like a family of mice."

"Mother!" Mom snatched the platter out of Gram's reach. "These are chicken liver paté from a recipe in *Gourmet* magazine. I spent all morning grinding up the livers and shaping them on the little crackers. Sometimes I wonder why I waste my time trying to do nice things for this family."

Gram lunged for the platter, grabbed two and

handed one to me. "Mmm. Delicious, don't you think, Kelly? Don't know how a terrible cook like me could have raised a fancy cook like your mother."

I didn't think they were so terrific, but I nodded just to keep out of an argument. I always got in a lot more trouble when Gram was around.

Mom smiled. "So, they taste good, even though they look like mice?"

Gram took another. "Oh, Ruth, I didn't mean anything. I was just making an observation, not an insult. Nothing wrong with mice. We have a whole family of them living with us."

"I don't know how you stand the little beasts," Mom said, arranging her casseroles on the table. "I wouldn't have rodents living in my house."

"Why not? You have Norm," Gram said, chuckling.

Dad folded his newspaper. "There's nothing worse than an old woman with a smart mouth. Unless it's an old woman with a smart mouth who happens to be your mother-in-law." He grinned at Gram. "How about passing me some of those mice, old woman."

"Dice?" Gramps said, appearing suddenly behind Dad. "You got a game goin', Norm? I'm in, as long as you're not playin' for more than nickels. Them quarter games are too rich for my blood."

"Oh, for heaven's sake," Mom said. "Everybody sit down so I can serve this meal. Everything is probably cold by now."

Gram pulled out a package of marshmallow salad from the deli and slid it across the table. "It's a picnic, Ruth. Everything's supposed to be cold. That's why we don't bring our stoves."

Mom ignored Gram and began unwrapping her casseroles one by one, folding each piece of aluminum foil into a neat square before putting it back in the picnic basket. She'd still be using those same pieces of foil at next year's Labor Day picnic. That's how organized Mom is. "The orchestra members are already warming up. Now we'll have to wolf down our food," she said, sighing again.

Gram squinted at the bandstand. "That's just George Kendricks. He's practicing, not warming up. The only time he picks up that old trumpet is right before a performance. He hasn't changed a bit since we were in high school together. Doesn't play any better than he did then, either."

It was hard to imagine that Gram was the same age as the old geezer trying to coax a note out of his trumpet on the bandstand. Gram's reddish-blonde hair had only turned partly gray, and it was long—almost to her waist. She always wore it in a thick braid, sometimes wrapped around her head, like today, and sometimes hanging down her back. Mom said a woman Gram's age should get a respectable hairdo, but I thought it looked great. Gram reminded me of Rapunzel in the book of fairy tales she gave me when I was little. Mom's hair was the same color as Gram's, only without the gray. The way she wore it, short and permed, almost made her look older than Gram.

Mom kept passing dish after dish until we were all stuffed. She really was a terrific cook. If they had a national casserole champion, she'd be it. You had to be fast when Mom started cleaning up, though, especially if you were a slow eater. Gramps had to spear his last deviled egg with a knife, just as Mom whipped his plate into a plastic garbage bag.

"I'm going to look for Rebecca and Lisa before the concert starts," I said.

Mom looked up. "It'll be getting dark soon. Don't go wandering off. And be sure to find us before the end of the concert. I don't want to get caught in the traffic jam."

Gram laughed. "Ruth, there aren't enough cars in this whole town to make a traffic jam. I swear, you look for things to worry about." She hugged me again. "If I don't see you later, Kelly, have a great time in school tomorrow."

"Don't tell her that," Mom said. "Kelly has to get serious about her schoolwork now. It's time she started thinking about what she wants to be when she grows up. When Robin was this age, she already knew she wanted to be a nutritionist."

My sister Robin is in her freshman year at college, and she probably knew she wanted to be a nutritionist when she was three weeks old. She's always been better than me in everything but picking slugs off Gram's cabbage plants. I thought my life would get better when she left, but for the week that she'd been gone, Mom had managed to fit her into the conversation at least six times a day. Robin was getting more and more perfect in Mom's mind. By the time she came home for Thanksgiving, she'd have a halo around her head and little bumps under the back of her sweater where her wings were sprouting.

Gram rescued the last of her Fritos just as Mom was about to ditch them. "Don't worry about Kelly's career plans, Ruth. I still haven't decided what *I'm* going to be when I grow up."

"That," Mom said, burping the lid on a Tupperware bowl, "is exactly my point."

Mom and Gram could never be together more than half an hour before they started slipping insults into their conversation. Dad told me it went back to the time when Mom was a kid and Gram ran off to New York for a while to be an actress. They never talked about it, but you could tell Mom had never forgiven Gram. Now Mom was getting even by picking away at every little thing Gram did. Sometimes I wished Mom would just go to a shrink and get it over with. Gram might have had her bad points, but she had more than enough good ones to make up for them.

Dad and Gramps had gone to get seats for the concert, and Mom and Gram were warming up to another fight. I didn't want to get caught in the crossfire, so I climbed over the picnic table bench and made my escape.

CHAPTER 2

The air was still warm, even though the sun had dipped below the trees. Crowds of people milled around the town park, but I couldn't recognize anybody in the weird light from the strings of colored Japanese lanterns. I always loved the Labor Day picnic. It was sort of sad, being the end of summer, but it was the only time the whole town got together to celebrate.

"Kelly! Over here!" Lisa and Rebecca were calling me from the hill behind the bandstand. I scrambled up the slope and settled down next to them on the squishy carpet of pine needles.

"You guys all ready for tomorrow?" I asked.

"I've tried on about a dozen outfits," Rebecca whined. "Could you two come over after the concert and help me decide?"

"We helped you decide two days ago," Lisa

said. "I thought it was the new jeans and the light blue sweater."

Rebecca wrinkled her nose. "The first day is such a big deal, especially in the middle school. Maybe I should wear that new red shirt. It's supposed to be hot tomorrow. What do you think, Kelly?"

Clothes weren't my thing, although I'd spent half the summer looking through Rebecca's collection of *Teen Scene* magazines, trying to act interested. "I think we should forget about what we're going to wear tomorrow and do something to make tonight truly memorable."

"Like what?" Lisa asked.

"Remember when we were little, and we used to run all over the park in the dark while our parents listened to the orchestra concert?"

Lisa rolled her eyes. "Oh, that's a great idea, Kelly. We can run all over the park making fools of ourselves."

"I don't mean we should really run around. We should think of something else that's as much fun."

Rebecca cracked her gum. "I don't get it."

As the orchestra burst forth with "Stars and Stripes Forever," an idea was slowly forming in my mind. "Tomorrow our whole lives are going to change when we walk through the door to Riverton Junior High, right?"

They both nodded.

I stood up. "Then tonight is our last chance to commit a truly childish act before we launch into adulthood."

"Just what do you have in mind?" Lisa was interested. I could tell by the look in her eyes.

"We have almost a whole package of balloons left from Robin's going-away-to-college party. They're in the back seat of the car."

"So?" Rebecca said. "I still don't get it." This didn't surprise me. Rebecca never "got" anything.

"You know how the percussion section sits in the back?" I said. "They stand up when they have to play, then sit down again."

"Yeah . . . so?" Lisa had a sneaky little smile.

"We fill the balloons with water and slip them on their chairs while they're standing up. Then, when they finish and sit down . . ."

"I love it!" Lisa said. "Let's get started."

Rebecca squinted at the bandstand. "They sit down and what?"

"Think about it, Rebecca," I said.

A look of understanding passed briefly over Rebecca's face, which was a sight you didn't see very often. "But what if we get caught?"

Lisa took her arm. "Nobody's going to get caught. Besides, who would believe we did it? We've always been the goody-goodies of Wilbur Rachet Elementary."

I took Rebecca's other arm. "Are you with us, Rebecca? Lisa and I can do it without you if you're chicken."

"All right. I'm in," she mumbled.

Lisa grinned and stuck out her hand. We did our secret triple handshake and headed for the parking lot. I dug around in the back seat of the car and found the balloons—eight of them. We went to a faucet where nobody could see us and took turns filling balloons and tying them off.

"Hurry up," Lisa said. "It's getting dark. They'll be doing the *1812 Overture* with fireworks pretty soon."

We discovered that we could only carry two balloons each without dropping them, so we settled for six. I finished up my last balloon, and we ran for the hill. I felt just the way I used to when we were little. There was still something exciting about running around with my best friends after dark.

When we got to the bandstand, we gathered for a last-minute conference. "There are only five players," Rebecca said. "We have too many balloons."

"The girl is a math genius," I said. "Don't worry about it, Rebecca. What we have to do is stay down in the shadows and get right up behind the percussion section. I'll peek up over the edge, and when I see that they're all standing up, I'll signal the two of you. Lisa, you take the timpanist and bass drummer. Rebecca, you get the xylophonist. And I'll do the snare drummer and the guy with the cymbals."

Rebecca made a face. "What's a xylo... whatever you said."

"Just put your balloon on the middle chair," Lisa said, rolling her eyes at me.

"Come on," I said. "Three of them are standing up already."

We ducked down so the portable spotlight didn't hit us as we edged toward the back of the bandstand. I could hear the snare drums and the xylophone, and when I peeked over the edge of the bandstand, I could see that the only percussionist still sitting was the timpani player. Then the music got faster and louder, and he got up, too.

"This is it!" I hissed to the others. Lisa and I placed our balloons on the chairs, but Rebecca was hanging back. I poked her, and she jumped up, shoving her balloon barely onto the middle chair. We scrambled back to the safety of the shadows on the hill, then circled around behind a group of people sitting toward the side of the bandstand. We had a perfect view of the percussionists' faces from there.

I saw the xylophonist put down his mallets and bend forward. "Look. He's sitting down," I whispered. "Watch his face."

He sat.

We watched.

Nothing happened.

Lisa nudged me. "What's wrong?"

"Maybe he's wearing thick pants," Rebecca volunteered.

We watched a few minutes longer, but the man's expression never changed.

"I don't understand it," I said. "Maybe he's been sitting up there so long, he's numb."

Lisa giggled. "Yeah, he has a dead end!"

"Come on, let's see what's going on." I started around to the back of the bandstand again, with Lisa and Rebecca following me. The xylophonist was leaning forward, turning the pages of the piece on his music stand.

"Look at that!" Rebecca said.

He was sitting just on the front part of a green balloon, and the rest of it was bulging ominously from under the seat of his pants. "I knew you had that balloon too far back on the chair," I whispered to Rebecca.

Suddenly the piece was over, and the xylophonist stood up to take a bow with the rest of the orchestra. The balloon quivered in the spotlight for a second like a round blob of lime Jell-O. Then they all sat down at once. It looked like Niagara Falls.

The skinny guy with the cymbals felt the water first. Then the snare drummer jumped up and grabbed the seat of his pants. The xylophonist looked over his shoulder and kept turning around in circles, like a dog trying to catch his tail. The big timpani player got up, felt the seat of his chair and picked up the remains of his balloon. Then he turned around and shaded his eyes, peering out into the darkness of our hill.

"He sees us," Rebecca squeaked.

"Maybe not," I said. "Don't move."

The orchestra leader must not have noticed what was going on, because he started the *1812 Overture.* Just as the music began, the timpani player jumped off the back of the bandstand and headed up the hill.

"Okay, move!" I shoved Rebecca ahead of me, and the three of us scrambled over the top of the hill. It was pitch dark, and pine branches kept hitting me in the face as we clung to each other and tried to keep moving. "Head for that light over there," I said. We stumbled and lurched through a small gully that came out at the other side of the picnic grounds.

When we got out front again, the timpani player was back in his place, and the orchestra was just getting to the good part where you could start to hear the cannons.

"I'm a mess," Rebecca said, brushing pine needles off her jeans.

"Forget it," I said. "You're also alive. Did you see the look on that guy's face? If he'd caught us . . ."

I thought I saw the timpani player glaring at us, but he was so far away, I couldn't tell for sure. He seemed to be pounding his drum a little harder than necessary, though. Nobody in the percussion section looked very happy.

"I told you we might get caught," Rebecca whispered.

"Yeah, but we didn't." Lisa grinned, then her expression changed. "Rebecca! Why didn't you get rid of the evidence?"

The unused water balloon, a bright yellow one that almost glowed in the dark, was in Rebecca's hands.

"Shhh!" A lady in front of us turned around and gave us a dirty look.

Rebecca shoved the balloon behind her back and looked around frantically for a place to put it. Then she set the balloon on the ground and sat on it. It took a second or two before any of us, including Rebecca, realized what she had done.

"Oooh. I don't believe I did that," Rebecca wailed. We tried not to laugh, but then we all started snorting, which was even worse. The lady in front of us was just starting to turn around again when the fireworks began. The noise muffled our laughter, and we stretched out on the grass to watch the sky explode over our heads. My favorite fireworks were the kind that expanded into a perfect circle, especially the blue ones. The booms shook the ground beneath us.

Lisa shouted over the music and noise. "It's going to be just glorious, isn't it?"

"The fireworks?" Rebecca asked.

"No. Junior high. Then high school. Then college. It's going to be so exciting."

"And the three of us will all stick together, just like always," I yelled.

In the bursts of light overhead, I could see the future Kelly, Lisa, and Rebecca. My daydream voice mumbled in my ear. It always sounds like the guy on TV who tells you what's going on in a golf tournament—the one who whispers into the mike with his voice low and gravelly.

Here they are, ladies and gentlemen, the three most popular, most beautiful, most talented and most brilliant students Riverton Junior High has ever seen, stunning in their matching red and yellow Riverton cheerleader outfits. This is the first time in history that Riverton has ever had three co-captains of the squad, but it's impossible to choose among these three outstanding students who have been inseparable since kindergarten. They're coming out in front of the crowd now, with the rest of the cheerleading squad behind them. It looks as if they might be ready to . . . yes, they are. Lisa, Rebecca, and Kelly are going to lead a cheer. The crowd is going wild.

"Two, four, six, eight.
Who do we appreciate?
Riverton! Riverton!
Yeaaaaaay!"

In the magic of the moment, with the music and the colored lanterns and fireworks, I believed it all. That was my first mistake.

CHAPTER 3

The worst part about junior high was trying to do the combination on my locker. I was still having trouble with it in the second week of school. Rebecca started bugging me. "Hurry up, Kelly. Lisa's waiting for us in the front hall."

I yanked on the lock, but it didn't budge. "Hang on. This thing is driving me nuts. It's made me late for three classes this week."

Rebecca leaned against the locker next to mine. "I can't remember that many numbers, so I just leave mine open. It saves a lot of time."

"Gee, that's brilliant, Rebecca. You could save even more time by leaving your stuff in a pile in the middle of the hall."

Rebecca scowled. "Don't be silly. Somebody might step on it." It was no fun using sarcasm on Rebecca.

"Isn't it exciting being in junior high?" she

asked. "I'm really upset that you don't have a single class with Lisa and me, though."

"You're upset!" I started the combination for the fourth time. "How do you think I feel? Most of the kids in my classes went to Arnold Harper Elementary. They all know each other, and the only person I know is Michael Granby."

Rebecca wrinkled her nose. "He's a creep. Don't you just love going to a different classroom for each subject? Sitting in one room all day used to get so boring."

"Yeah," I said. "It's great." Actually I hated all that running around. I'd give anything to be back in my old seat at Wilbur Rachet. I knew why Rebecca liked it, though. School ranked pretty low on her list of favorite things, somewhere between taking out the garbage and having her braces tightened. For her, any distraction was welcome, even if it was just wandering around in the hall, getting lost.

Rebecca cracked her gum in my ear. "If you're going to take forever with that lock, I'm going to meet Lisa, so she won't think we left without her. We'll wait for you in the front hall."

"Okay." Without Rebecca breathing over my shoulder, I was able to give the lock my full concentration, and after three more tries it opened.

I ran down the front staircase and found Rebecca and Lisa waiting for me by the door. A crowd of students clustered around the main bulletin board.

"What's all the excitement about?" I asked.

Lisa shrugged. "Tryouts for a play, I think. Come on. Let's get out of here."

"No, wait," I said. I pushed my way into the crowd until I could read the sign: Auditions for *Cinderella*. I read all the small print, then worked my way back to Lisa and Rebecca. "Hey, this is it, guys—our first project in junior high."

Lisa looked suspicious. "Is this going to be another one of your dumb ideas?"

I ignored her remark. "The school drama club is having auditions for *Cinderella* tomorrow after school."

Rebecca made a face. "*Cinderella?* Who wants to do a play for little kids?"

"But, Rebecca," I said, "just imagine what the costumes will be like. I mean, there's a royal ball and everything."

"Oh, Lisa, Kelly's right. Let's try out. We'll get to wear ball gowns." Rebecca was practically in orbit. After being best friends since kindergarten, I knew how to zero in on her weak spots.

Lisa wasn't as easy to convince. "I don't care what we get to wear. It's still a play for little kids. We're supposed to be adults now, remember?"

I grabbed Lisa's arm and pulled her away from the crowd. "Don't you see? We've spent more than a week at this school, and we haven't found a way to fit in. This is perfect! It's much easier to get to know people when you're working on a project together. It gives you something to talk about."

Lisa yanked her arm out of my grip. "The only people you'll be getting to know are the class jerks."

"Please!" Rebecca whined, coming up next to us. "You have to try out with us. It wouldn't be the same without you. We've always done everything together."

"Besides," I said, "if Rebecca and I are busy with the play, who will you hang around with? You don't want to be a loner, do you?" Bingo! Weak spot!

"Oh, all right," Lisa said. "I'll do it. Let me see this poster." The crowd had cleared away now. "Oh, look. Mr. Foland is the drama club adviser, and he's directing the play."

"Who's he?" Rebecca asked.

"Our English teacher. You know, the one with the beard."

"Oh yeah. He's cute. Nice, too." Rebecca squinted at the poster. "This says you start out with singing auditions for the chorus and then the best people will get to read for the lead parts. What are we supposed to sing? I don't know any songs from *Cinderella.*"

"I think you can sing 'My Country 'Tis of Thee' or something," I said. "They just want to hear what kind of voice you have."

Lisa's eyes grew wide. "I can't get up in front of a whole room of people and sing."

"Sure you can," I said. "It's simple. You just have to look as if you have complete confidence in yourself. It fakes out the judges every time. Trust me. I know it works." I wasn't exactly lying. The old fake-out had worked for me in second grade, when I got the part of the only singing tulip in the Spring Garden Pageant. That was my first and only performance.

Suddenly I remembered how Mom felt about plays, and I was pretty sure she wouldn't be wild about me trying out for one. I should have thought of that before I opened my big mouth. Maybe it wasn't too late to steer Lisa and Rebecca in another direction. "Look, if you're really scared about the audition," I said, "we can find something else to join. Sports, maybe."

"You know I hate sports," Rebecca said. "The play sounds like much more fun."

"Well, Lisa said she didn't want to audition. I

don't think we should make her do something she's afraid of."

"I never said I was afraid. I've just never done anything like that before. Who knows, it might be fun. Let's shake on it." She held out her hand, and we all did the secret handshake.

Now I was stuck, and even though Mom might not approve, I'd have to find a way to be in the play. As we walked home, my daydream voice started mumbling in my ear.

Kelly MacDonald is walking up to the piano with confidence. She's turning toward the judges and smiling. The music is starting, and Kelly's voice rings out flawless and clear. One of the judges is writing something on her sheet. Let's see if we can look over her shoulder to see what it is. "Kelly MacDonald—excellent poise and grace." The other judge writes, "I have never heard a more thrilling rendition of 'My Country 'Tis of Thee'." It looks as if Kelly MacDonald is well on her way to another stunning victory.

CHAPTER 4

"Mom, I may be a little late coming home from school tomorrow," I said as I was clearing the supper dishes.

"Why is that?" Mom asked.

"Lisa, Rebecca, and I are going to...um... join one of the after-school clubs."

I gritted my teeth, waiting for her to ask which one. "That's nice, dear. Clubs are a good way to meet people. That's how Robin became so popular. Just make sure it doesn't interfere with your homework."

"Oh, it won't, Mom. I'll make sure of that." I couldn't believe it. She never asked which club, so it was almost like she was giving me permission. Not quite, but almost.

I spent most of the next day running and re-running my audition daydream, with slight variations and embellishments. About halfway through last period, the bell rang, and an announcement came over the loudspeaker. Harvey DeMott grabbed his books and bolted out of his seat, because he'd been asleep and thought it was the final bell. He wasn't any more disappointed than I was.

Mr. Wilson, the principal, sounded like a robot over the crackly P.A. system. "All students interested in auditioning for the Drama Club's production of *Cinderella* should report to the music room immediately following the final bell. Singing auditions will be held in the music room, followed by dramatic auditions in the auditorium."

The rest of the period was a total loss. My throat began to feel dry, so I slipped a stick of gum out of my purse. Mrs. Cronin absolutely went into orbit if we chewed gum in class, but this was an emergency. Besides, I was pretty good at just chewing when her back was turned. The rest of the time, I kept it tucked in my cheek.

After about a hundred years the final bell rang. I practically flew down the hall to my locker, ready to do battle with it. The rattle and slamming of all the other locker doors wasn't helping my concentration any. I forced myself to slow down. Twenty-five right...left past twenty-five to sixteen ... right to forty-three. Finally! Just as the door swung open, a hand reached past me and slammed it shut. My books scattered all over the floor.

"Michael Granby, I'm going to kill you!" I shouted. He grinned and waved as he retreated backward down the hall.

Michael had turned up in all but one of my classes, and I couldn't stand him. He was always teasing me, like a brother. I almost hadn't recognized him when I first saw him this fall. We'd been about the same height in fifth grade, but now he towered over me by at least six inches. He was all awkward arms and legs, like a marionette.

Now I was going to be late for the audition. I hoped Lisa and Rebecca had saved me a seat. After two more tries, the locker opened. I dumped all the books I didn't need for homework in the locker and slammed it shut.

When I got to the music room, there were already a dozen people ahead of me. Lots of them were older kids. I hadn't thought about having to compete with them.

Mrs. Hattersley, the music teacher, was taking names at the door. I spotted Lisa and Rebecca in the last row and slipped into the seat they'd saved between them.

"Kelly, I'm so scared I think I'm going to throw up," Lisa whispered. "I don't know why I let you talk me into these things." She looked pale, and the possibility of her throwing up made my own stomach lurch.

"You don't have anything to worry about," Rebecca said. "But look at me. I'm dressed all wrong for this. Do you think I have time to run home quick and change?"

"No," I said. "You're fine. Look, we all can sing pretty well, so there's no problem. Just don't let them see that you're nervous. That's the kiss of death."

Mrs. Hattersley was at the piano now, talking to Miss Goodrupp, the accompanist. We'd heard about Miss Goodrupp long before we moved up to junior high. She looked old and stiff until she started to play. Then, when she played a fast piece, she kept tightening the muscles of her rear end in time to the music. It made her jiggle up and down, like a baby being bounced on its mother's knee. I don't think she knew she was doing it because she usually had her eyes closed when she played. It cracked us up in music class, especially when she played "The Battle Hymn of the Republic."

"All right, everybody. Let's get started." Mrs. Hattersley's voice squeaked when she tried to talk over all the noise. "I'm delighted to see so many of you here. Please come up to Miss Goodrupp when your name is called. Meg Hammond, you're first."

Mrs. Hattersley took her seat in the front row next to two teachers I didn't know. They all had clipboards and pencils, so I figured they must be judges. A girl went up to the front and handed her music to Miss Goodrupp. Then she came around to the front of the piano and stood in that curved-in space with her right arm resting on the piano lid. She looked really cool and professional, like a nightclub singer. I'd have to remember that when it was my turn. Then she nodded to Miss Goodrupp to start. I'd have to remember that too. I figured by the time it was my turn, I'd have learned a lot of things I could add to my performance. It was the little things that counted with the judges.

Rebecca leaned over and whispered in my ear. "That girl is in ninth grade with my sister. I love her outfit. You know, I have something almost like that at home. That's what I should have worn."

"Shhh!" I whispered. "I want to hear her."

Meg Hammond had a great voice. Her song sounded like something from a Broadway show, and she smiled a lot when she sang. Everybody clapped when she finished. Mrs. Hattersley called her over and talked to her for a minute. I couldn't make out what they were saying, but then Meg gathered up her things and went out the door to the auditorium.

The next four or five people were okay, but nobody was as good as Meg had been. There was one kid who did a funny song about junk food. Everybody laughed a lot, and he got tons of applause when he finished. I thought he'd made up the song himself, but Lisa said she heard it once on the radio.

The next person to try out was Brenda Schrader, a girl from my homeroom. She sounded pretty good, but the song she'd chosen was "Zip-a-dee-doo-dah," which was real peppy. Old Galloping Goodrupp really got bouncing on that one, and you could hear snickering all over the room. Poor Brenda thought everyone was laughing at her, and her voice got thin and wavery at the end. When she finished, Mrs. Hattersley told us that anyone who couldn't behave would have to leave the room. I guess she'd never noticed how Miss Goodrupp played, although I didn't know how anyone could miss it. Anyway, Brenda looked ready to cry when she left, and I felt sorry for her. Tomorrow, in homeroom, I'd have to tell her it was Miss Goodrupp everybody was laughing at, not her.

There were some pretty boring people after that, and I tuned out for a while. I replayed my audition daydream a few times. I even tried one version where I wasn't going to try out at all, but they couldn't find a Cinderella and dragged me in to audition. Naturally I got the part.

Kelly MacDonald has just been offered the role of Cinderella, but she seems to be refusing it. Let's see if we can hear what's being said. Mr. Foland is kissing her hand.

"Kelly, you're perfect for the part. The play will be a smash hit with you in the starring role."

Kelly is subtly withdrawing her hand. "You're being too kind, Mr. Foland. But you see, I really can't accept the role. Surely there are others who could play the part as well."

The other students are gathering around Kelly, pleading with her.

"We need you, Kelly."

"Yeah. Nobody else has your talent."

"Please, Kelly. You have to say yes."

Mr. Foland is taking Kelly's arm and leading her to a chair on the edge of the stage. He's pulling something out of his pocket. I can't make out what it is . . . the light is catching it . . . is it? . . . could it be? . . . Yes!

Ladies and gentlemen, Mr. Foland is holding a dazzling glass slipper. He's . . . he's kneeling down. He's slipping it on her foot. Will it fit? We'll know in a second. Yes, the glass slipper is a perfect fit!

Mr. Foland is standing now, bowing to Kelly. "There. It's decided! Ladies and gentlemen, may I present your Cinderella, Kelly MacDonald."

Wait. Kelly is motioning to the crowd to stop applauding. "All right. I'll do it, but only under one condition."

"Anything," *Mr Foland says.* "Your wish is my command."

Now Kelly is leading Mr. Foland offstage. She's limping slightly as she walks with one dazzling high-heeled slipper. She's whispering something to him, but we can't make it out from here. They seem to have reached some agreement. Yes, Kelly has consented to be Cinderella. The other students are cheering and running up to hug her.

Mr. Foland is heading this way. Let's see if we can find out what Kelly's condition was.

Mr. Foland, would you come up to the microphone for a minute?

"Certainly."

Could you tell us what was said over there? What did Kelly want before she'd play the part of Cinderella? Did she ask for a tremendous amount of money?

"No. She wants no money at all. She merely asked that I find parts in the play for her two dear lifelong friends, Lisa and Rebecca."

Did you hear that, ladies and gentlemen? Not only is Kelly MacDonald beautiful and talented, but she's generous and thoughtful as well.

This plot was a little too unrealistic, even for a daydream, so I went back to my more sensible version. I was just getting to the part where I start to sing, when I felt Rebecca's elbow in my ribs.

"Kelly MacDonald? Are you ready?" Mrs. Hattersley was looking around the room for me.

I stood up too fast, and my books all crashed to the floor. I pretended it hadn't happened. I was going to keep cool, no matter what. I walked slowly to the front of the room, fit myself into the curve of the piano and placed my right arm casually on the lid. None of the other kids after Meg had done this. It paid to be observant. I smiled and nodded to Miss Goodrupp.

She wasn't smiling back. "The music," she whispered.

I nodded again. Of course I wanted her to play the music. Actually I had debated that, after Brenda, but how bouncy could she get on "My Country..." Oh my gosh! She didn't know what I was going to sing! I felt my face get hot, and there was a sudden fluttery feeling in my chest. It couldn't be butterflies from being nervous, because I knew that was supposed to be in your stomach. This was high up, almost in my throat.

I heard some whispering going on in the room and a few giggles. Miss Goodrupp was clearing her throat.

"I'm doing 'My Country 'Tis of Thee,'" I whispered.

"What key?"

"I don't care. The regular one is fine."

I nodded again and she played a little introduction. I came in nice and loud, but Miss Goodrupp was playing something that didn't go with what I was singing.

"Let's try it again, Kelly," she said.

This time she plunked out my note real loud, and I came in right, but something awful happened. The voice that came out was tiny and shaky, not like mine at all. As soon as I heard it, I got that fluttering feeling again, but this time it was much stronger, pushing down on my chest.

I thought about Uncle Ralph, who'd had a heart attack last year. He said he had a pressure in his chest just before they took him to the hospital.

* * *

Authorities at Riverton Junior High report that Kelly MacDonald, outstanding sixth-grader, was struck down by a heart attack in the middle of an audition for...

I couldn't catch my breath. I stopped again. I looked up and saw Lisa. Her eyes were huge and her face was dead white. She looked like she was going to throw up any second.

A group of older kids were huddled together, whispering. Then they all laughed. Mrs. Hattersley stood up and shot them a look that shut them up.

"I'm sorry," I mumbled to Miss Goodrupp. "Could we start over?"

My heart was pounding so loud I could hear a squishing sound in my ears with each beat. I'd show these kids if it killed me.

...ending what promised to be a dazzling career. Ms. MacDonald is survived by her two lifelong friends...

I got back in my Meg Hammond position and tried to smile, but I could only get one side of my mouth to move. The muscles around my lips felt twitchy. Miss Goodrupp started the introduction again. Most of the kids were looking down at their laps, their shoulders shaking with laughter. I gritted my teeth and plunged in.

"My country 'tis of me." Oh no, did I say "'tis of me"?

"Sweet land of—" I couldn't get enough breath and had to sneak one in here.

"Lib-er"—another breath—"ty. Of thee I sing."

I struggled to take in enough air to get through the next line. When I tried to sing the word "land," it was too high, and no sound came out at all. There were muffled snorts and giggles coming from all over the room. Mrs. Hattersley had moved to the front corner and was shooting looks around the room like poison darts.

. . . several obnoxious Riverton Junior High students were killed earlier today when struck by darts containing an unknown substance . . .

I could feel the sweat running down under my arms, so I abandoned my Meg Hammond position and held my arms down tight to my sides. I wasn't even trying to smile anymore. I just wanted to finish and get out of there. I took one gigantic breath and did the whole last line real fast: "From e-ev-ry-y-mountainside-le-etfree-domring."

That took Miss Goodrupp by surprise, so I'd already reached my seat by the time she got to "ring." There was a lot of clapping and laughing. My science book had slid under the seat in front of me, and I had to drop to my hands and knees to get it out. Rebecca and Lisa didn't say anything. They just watched me with their mouths hanging open, like they were in shock or something. I gathered my stuff and ran out of the room. I could hear Mrs. Hattersley trying to quiet the kids as I ran down the hall.

I was ruined.

CHAPTER 5

My fingers were shaking so much, I couldn't even turn the dial on my locker, much less get the numbers right. I stopped without trying to finish the combination, took the main staircase steps two at a time and burst through the front door. Trees, houses, and people were all a blur as I raced down Cramer Avenue. My heart was pounding in my ears. Good! Maybe I'd have a heart attack after all. Then I could just drop dead and never have to talk to anybody again. I ran even harder until I came to our house.

I unlocked the front door, flew upstairs to the refuge of my room, and slammed the door behind me. I flopped on my bed and stared at the ceiling.

Every now and then a picture of the audition flashed through my mind. I could still hear the kids laughing. I must have looked so stupid up there, trying to be Meg Hammond.

I looked at the clock. Mom was due home from her gourmet cooking class any minute. I couldn't expect any sympathy if I told her I'd tried out for a play. This would just give her a chance to say, "I told you so." Gram would understand, though. She must have auditioned when she went to New York.

I went downstairs and left a note on the kitchen table, telling Mom I was going to the farm. Then I grabbed my bike and took off. It was only this past year that I'd been allowed to ride out to the farm because it was a seven-mile trip with a big hill at the end.

I made a detour through some back streets so I wouldn't have to ride past the school. The other kids might be getting out of the auditions by now. After I passed the diner at the edge of town, I started down the road that wound along the river. The trees at the top of Wheeler Hill were already beginning to turn red and gold. In a few weeks it would be a brilliant mass of color.

As I came around the last curve, I could see the farm on the crest of the hill. I turned up Wheeler Hill Road and shifted into a lower gear, but toward the end I slowed to a wobbly crawl and had to get off and walk my bike. I never could make it all the way to the top.

When I came to the long driveway lined with maple trees, I got back on and rode to the house.

It was an old farmhouse, over a hundred and fifty years old. People had added onto it over the years, so it grew in all directions. There was even a section that connected the house to the main barn. Gramps said they used to do that so the farmer wouldn't have to go out in the cold New England winter to milk the cows. That's where Gram had her stained-glass studio.

As my bike tires came to a crunching stop on the gravel driveway, Gramps came out of the barn, squinting in the bright sun.

"What brings you out here, Kelly? Anything wrong?"

"No, everything's fine, Gramps. I just felt like coming out."

"Running trout? Not this time of year. You got your seasons mixed up. Didn't even know you liked to fish. How are things going at your new school?"

"Great, Gramps."

He shook his head. "Late? That's no way to start out a new school. You'll have to get yourself up earlier in the morning. Why, when I was a boy, I had to have all the cows milked before I went to school. I had to get up at least by..."

I had to listen to Gramps as he launched into one of his stories. "If you want to see your grandmother, she's working as usual," Gramps finally said, pointing his thumb toward the studio. "Maybe you can get her to take a break. She works harder than a plow horse."

"Okay, I'll see what I can do." Just as I opened the studio door, Gram yelled, "Close that door!"

I slammed the door behind me, and Miranda, Gram's cat, skidded to a stop, carrying a small braided rug with her across the slippery floor.

"What's the matter?" I asked.

Gram looked up from her worktable. "Blasted cat got a bird this morning, so she's grounded for the day. We have mice around here by the carload, but oh no, she has to have birds."

"She's just doing what her instincts tell her to, Gram," I said.

"She'll have to learn to control herself. If I did everything my instincts told me to do, I'd be in jail." Gram leaned forward, arranging some pieces of green and blue glass on a clear plastic pattern. "I almost forgot, your mother called just before you got here. She said they'll pick you up later, if you don't want to ride your bike home. You're supposed to call when you're ready."

"I'll be ready about a week from Friday."

"Something wrong?"

"I messed up on my audition for the school play."

"Hmmm. That's too bad." She shoved a few pieces of glass around on the pattern, then sighed and leaned back in her chair. "Rats, this isn't going to fit again. If I have to cut these pieces one more time, I'll go bananas. I have to have a set of four stained-glass windows finished by the end of the month, and this is only the first one. This job seems to be getting harder as I get older."

"Maybe you should slow down and not do so many windows, Gram."

Gram's eyes flashed as she looked up. "And do what with my spare time? Cook and clean house like your mother?"

Looking around the studio with books, papers, and junk piled in every corner, I couldn't help thinking that a little cleaning wouldn't hurt, but I didn't say anything. If I had to make a choice, I'd rather live in Gram's house, where I could relax and be myself. At home, Mom always rushed in to "straighten up" as soon as I left a room. It almost seemed as if she didn't want any traces of me left around.

Gram went back to taping a pattern to a deep blue pane of glass and put on her safety goggles.

Then she dipped her cutter in kerosene and ran it firmly over the glass with a deep crunching sound. Gram picked up the pliers and snapped the glass perfectly along the scored line.

I could tell she was concentrating too hard to carry on a conversation, so I climbed up the spiral staircase to my favorite spot—a small open loft at the barn end of the studio. This was where Gram stored the scraps of stained glass that were big enough to save. A shaft of late afternoon sun shot through the skylight onto a small worktable that held a rainbow of glass pieces Gram had been arranging for a sun catcher. I sat down and held up different fragments, making colorful reflections fall on the white surface of the table.

Gram was still muttering over her glass cutter. At one point, she reached up and pulled the pins out of her hair, letting the heavy braid swing down her back. Then she messed up three cuts in a row, swept the shards into a special can for broken glass and left the room. She was just coming back in with a Dr. Pepper, when she looked up and saw me and almost dropped the bottle. "Kelly, you scared me! I forgot you were here."

"That's me, invisible," I said. Coming out here

wasn't such a great idea after all. Gram didn't even know I was alive.

She squinted up at me. "What did you say?"

I wound my way down the staircase. "Nothing. I think I'll go outside for a while. I'll see you later." Miranda shot past my feet as I went out the door, but Gram didn't notice. "Lay off the birds," I growled at the cat, as I kicked a big stone in the driveway.

Now I felt worse than ever. I'd been hoping Gram would find a way to make everything okay again, but she was too busy to care about what had happened to me. The hurt from the audition had settled itself into a hard lump in my stomach.

I followed the driveway past the big red barn, then opened the gate and headed up the hill. In the center of the upper meadow, like a queen holding court, stood a huge spreading oak tree, my climbing tree. I jumped up to catch the lowest limb and swung my feet around it. I followed my usual route, branch by branch, until I reached the spot where I could see the whole valley. The only sounds were the buzzing of insects and the distant bleating of some sheep working their way up a steep slope on the other side of the valley. I just sat there for a while,

soaking up the peaceful scene. I tried to forget
the fact that, by now, half the kids in that valley
were laughing at me. And the other half just
hadn't heard about the audition yet.

*Word is spreading...ha ha...about the ridiculous
performance...hee hee...put on by formerly
fantastic...ho ho ho...sixth-grader Kelly MacDonald at the auditions for...*

I cut off my daydream voice. If it couldn't say
something nice, I wasn't going to listen to it.
Gramps's dog, Rusty, broke the silence by
bounding up through the meadow to greet me.
He was obviously going to circle the tree and
bark until I climbed down to see him.

"You win, Rusty." I retraced my path through
the maze of branches and dropped to the
ground. Rusty danced in circles the whole time.

"It must be wonderful to live a dog's life. You
never have to audition for anything, do you?" I
sat next to him in the warm meadow grass and
scratched behind his ears. Rusty was the only
dog I ever met who could actually smile.

"Here, catch." For a second, I thought Rusty
had learned to talk, but I looked up just in time
to see Gram toss a shiny red apple to me.

I caught it. "Gram! I didn't hear you coming."

She settled down beside me on the grass and started polishing another apple with the bottom of her T-shirt. "That makes two of us who are having trouble hearing today. My mind was a million miles away back at the house, Kelly. What did you want to tell me?"

I took a deep breath and gave her a blow-by-blow description of the audition.

When I finished, Gram tossed her apple core into the tall meadow grass and wiped her mouth with the back of her hand. "That sounds pretty bad. How did Rebecca and Lisa do?"

"I didn't hang around to find out. I'll never be able to face either of them again, Gram. The worst part is, the whole thing was my idea. Lisa and Rebecca didn't even want to audition. I practically forced them into it."

"Did you practice what you were going to do for your audition?"

"No, I knew I could sing pretty well, so I thought I could fake it. Then I got in there and freaked out."

"Everyone gets stage fright at one time or another. That's no disgrace."

"Did you ever have stage fright when you went to New York to be an actress?"

A quick frown passed over Gram's face, and she ran her hand over a small patch of peppermint in the grass. As she plucked a few leaves and crushed them between her fingers, a sharp toothpaste smell surrounded us. "I've had it many times. Probably my worst case of it happened when I was about your age."

"Really? You were a child actress?"

Gram sniffed at the mint, then popped a leaf into her mouth. "No, it was a dance recital—the first year my teacher had given me a solo. I felt pretty important, but I didn't put much time into practicing the dance." She looked at me. "I had a tendency to do more daydreaming than working."

"There's going to be a moral to this story," I said. "I can feel it coming."

Gram smiled. "Well, anyway, I was full of confidence until the curtain opened. Then the music started, and after I did the first few steps, my mind went completely blank. I couldn't think of what came next."

"What did you do? Just stand there?"

"No. I kept repeating the same step over and over. It was a pas de chat, a jump from side to side with the feet picked up high, like this." She demonstrated, using her hands. "I didn't even think about smiling, so my face showed how terrified I was. Years later, my father told me that I'd looked like a grasshopper having an anxiety attack." She fell back in the grass, chuckling.

"At least you can laugh about what happened to you, Gram. I sure can't see anything funny about my audition."

"Of course you can't. You'll have to wait till the pain wears off." She propped herself up on one elbow. "Next time you audition for something, though, you'll know you should practice ahead of time."

"Yeah, I hear you," I said, "but there isn't going to be a next time. I'd never go through that again."

"You could find other ways to get involved in this play besides being in the chorus."

"Oh, sure. I'd planned to be Cinderella. That would've been nice."

"I'm not so sure. I've heard that glass slippers give you blisters." Gram wiggled her big toe through the hole in her sneaker. "I go for comfort, myself."

She studied me for a minute, the way she always did when she was coming up with an idea. "Seems like there's something else you could do for this play. You sew pretty well, and you've always been good in art. Why don't you work on the costumes or the sets? I did sets for a play when I was an art major in college and had a wonderful time."

"That's just not the same. If Lisa and Rebecca passed the audition, they'll be going to rehearsals all the time. I'd never even see them."

"I wish I had an easy answer for you," Gram said, getting to her feet, "but I'm afraid there isn't one." She offered me her hand and pulled me up. "Chalk it up to experience, kid. Come on, I have a whole mess of windows to do, and I could use some help."

When we got back to the studio, Gram ran a copper strip around a small rectangular piece of glass and handed it to me. "Here, smooth this out over the edges of the glass with the fid. I'll grind the edges on a few more pieces for you."

I took the small wooden tool and rubbed the creases out of the thin sheet of copper, making sure it fit tight against the glass. If there were any gaps when Gram soldered the pieces together, it would cause a weakness in the finished window. Gram had let me "play" stained glass since I was little, but lately she was letting me help once in a while on a real project. I moved over to avoid getting hit from the water spray as she turned on the grinder.

"You know what I liked about designing sets, Kelly?" Gram shouted over the noise of the grinder. "I created a miniature world on paper, then made it into a life-size world on the stage. It was like being able to walk into my own drawing."

I nodded without saying anything. I knew Gram meant well, but she just didn't understand. Nobody did.

CHAPTER 6

The next morning, I waited for Lisa and Re-becca on our front steps. They both seemed surprised to see me. Rebecca whispered something to Lisa.

Lisa shushed her and looked embarrassed. "Hi, Kelly. I called you last night, and your dad told me you'd gone out to the farm."

"Are you okay?" Rebecca asked. "We were really worried about you after..." Lisa stopped her with an elbow in the ribs.

"Oh yeah, the audition," I said. We walked along in silence for about half a block. I looked at Rebecca and Lisa out of the corner of my eye. They felt sorry for me, and being pitied was even worse than being laughed at. It was time for the old fake-out. "Hey, you two don't think that was for real, do you? My audition act?"

Lisa's mouth dropped open. "Your act? You

mean you were just pretending to goof up?"

"Sure. I couldn't resist playing it for laughs. The whole thing seemed so stupid."

"How could you do that?" Rebecca said. "You wrecked our chances for being in the play together."

"Wait a minute, Rebecca," Lisa said. "I'm not sure Kelly messed up on purpose. Maybe she's just bluffing to cover up because she conned us into auditioning and then messed up."

I didn't have time to think of a comeback, because as we started up the sidewalk to the school, we could see a big crowd around the front hall bulletin board.

Lisa clutched my arm. "The list must be posted."

"Oh, I can't stand it," Rebecca squealed. "What if we didn't make it? I'll just die." They ran ahead, but I kept walking at the same speed. I knew I didn't need to look for my name on the list.

As I went through the front door, Lisa and Rebecca were jumping up and down and hugging each other. So they made it. Big deal. It was only a stupid play.

I slipped around behind the crowd and headed for the stairs. I almost escaped, but Rebecca grabbed my arm. "Kelly, Lisa got a lead part. Can you believe it? She's the only sixth-grader who got a lead—the part of Portia. Isn't that fantastic? And I made it into the chorus."

"Rebecca, you're yelling in my ear," I said, shaking loose from her grip. "Who's Portia, anyway?"

"One of the best parts. Portia is one of the mean stepsisters."

I hadn't expected that. I thought they both might make the chorus, but I never dreamed either of them could get a lead. Lisa was coming toward me with a big smile on her face. I couldn't stand it. "Perfect!" I said. "They certainly believe in typecasting."

They both stood watching me with their mouths hanging open as I ran up the stairs.

A bunch of kids were laughing in the corner of homeroom. When they saw me, they broke up to go to their seats. I'd forgotten that some of them had been in the audition yesterday. By now, even the ones who hadn't been there must know about me.

As if that weren't bad enough, I looked up and saw Michael Granby coming over to me. I wasn't in the mood for his teasing today. I'd really given him some ammunition this time. I braced myself for his attack.

He had a funny expression on his face, not

the usual stupid grin. He leaned down and spoke in a quiet voice I'd never heard before. "I really felt for you in that audition, Kelly. Are you okay?"

I waited for the punch line, but none came. He was just looking at me with a kind of shy, concerned expression.

"Yeah, I'm all right. Thanks," I mumbled. I was so surprised, I didn't even use my story about playing it for laughs. Michael grinned and gave me a thumbs-up sign as he went back to his desk.

First-period science really dragged on. Mr. DeVries was drawing stupid little things with weird names on the board, and we were supposed to be copying them into our notebooks. I did the amoeba and the paramecium, but when I got to the hydra, I messed it up and had to start on a fresh page.

The second time I drew it, it looked a little bit like a dragon, so I made flames coming out of its mouth. Then I drew a castle behind it with a moat and drawbridge. I did the main part of the castle like an X-ray, so I could show what was inside. I made it look like the castle ballroom scene in my old fairy tale book. I used to spend hours looking at that book, pretending I could walk into the pictures—imagining I was wan-

dering through the halls of the castle or exploring the enchanted forest.

I suddenly realized that if I designed the sets
for the play, it could be just like Gram had said. I
could draw the castle ballroom, then make it life
size on the stage so that I could walk right into it,
the way I always wanted to.

I was concentrating on drawing the turrets of
the castle, making little square indentations in
the wall, when I sensed somebody watching me.
That's when I looked up into the eyes of Mr.
DeVries.

He took my notebook and studied the picture
closely. "Your hydra is a bit unusual, Kelly. A
mutation, perhaps? And the environment is
much too elaborate. They prefer swamp water
to castles." He showed my picture to the whole
class, and everybody laughed. Mr. DeVries never
had to use detention for punishment. He just
embarrassed kids to death.

"You're a talented artist, Kelly," he said, putting the notebook down on my desk, "but let's
concentrate on less exotic forms of one-celled
creatures for the rest of the period, shall we?"

This got another big laugh from the class, but
I didn't pay any attention to it. Mr. DeVries had
called me a talented artist, and he wasn't the
kind of teacher to throw compliments around.

That settled it. I had study hall second period, and I'd use the time to make sketches for the sets.

Before the bell even rang for the beginning of study hall, I opened my science notebook to a clean page and started to work. I could picture the way I wanted the drawings to look in color, but all I had was a pencil. By the end of the period, though, I had three pretty good sketches. I had to get them to Mr. Foland and let him know I wanted to do the set designs.

I went to Mr. Foland's classroom right before lunch. I figured there wouldn't be any students in the room then. There weren't, but there wasn't any Mr. Foland in the room either. I hung around, looking at the Broadway show posters hanging all over the walls. After about ten minutes, I decided to leave the drawings on his desk with a note. I was just starting to get the drawings out of my notebook when Mr. Foland came in.

"Are you looking for me?" he asked.

"Oh, you scared me. I wanted to see you to show you ... I mean I have these sketches that I ..." As I pulled the sketches out of my notebook, the ring clasp let go, scattering papers all over the floor.

Mr. Foland darted around, catching papers as

they slid across the room. I stood there like an idiot, watching him. He looked like somebody out of a Shakespearean play, tall and thin, with one of those close-clipped beards. "There, I think you're back together again," he said, handing me a jumbled pile of papers. "How can I help you? First of all, I don't think we've met. You're not one of my students, are you?"

Why did I always have to mess up when I was trying to make an impression on somebody? I'd been thinking he knew me because of my audition daydream. I could feel my face getting hot.

My words came tumbling out. "I'm Kelly Mac-Donald, from Mrs. Isaacs' sixth-grade homeroom. I want to do the scenery for *Cinderella,* and I have some sketches here. I know I can do a good job. I'm pretty good in art." I shoved the sketches across the desk and held my breath.

Mr. Foland studied each one carefully, then spread them all out in front of him on the desk. "You *are* good in art, Kelly. Quite good, in fact."

"These are just black and white," I explained. "I didn't have time to do them in color, but that's what really makes the difference. That's how you put the magic in it, to make it look like it's all happening in an enchanted place." In my mind I could see the way I wanted it to look, with rich colors, like Gram's stained glass.

"That's a pretty sophisticated concept for someone your age, Kelly. Have you studied art?"

"Well, I've had art in school, but most of it I've learned from my grandmother, I guess. She's an artist, and I've spent a lot of time with her. And she's taken me to quite a few galleries and art shows."

"Oh, really? What's your grandmother's name?"

"Well, she's not famous or anything. She works in stained glass, mostly, but she paints, too, once in a while."

Just then the bell rang and ended our conversation. "Leave your sketches with me and I'll give them to Mr. Sampson, Kelly. I'm directing *Cinderella,* but he's the producer, so the final decision will be his. I'll get back to you on Monday."

As I hurried down the hall to my next class, my feet barely touched the floor. I didn't even care that I'd missed lunch and I'd probably starve to death before last period. I'd finally found my place in this school. I was going to be doing something that mattered, and I felt wonderful.

CHAPTER 7

I called Gram Saturday morning to tell her I was going to do the scenery. She came right over with some of her art supplies and helped me get set up on the kitchen table.

"You're going to have a great time with this," Gram said, splurting some red paint onto a palette. She didn't remind me that it was her idea in the first place, but I could tell she was pleased.

"This isn't as easy as I thought it would be, Gram. I know what I want it to look like, but I'm not sure how to get it on paper."

"That's the beauty of acrylic paint. The paint dries fast, and if it's not the way you want it, you can paint over it. You can either use it with a lot of water like this . . ." Gram wet a piece of paper and pulled a pale pink wash across it with her brush. "Or you can use it straight from the tube, like oil paint." She crumpled up a paper towel and dabbed at a blob of paint that had dripped on the kitchen table. "If you get stuck, just close your eyes and picture it in your mind the way you want it to be. That always helps me."

Just then, Mom came in with a load of groceries. "Where on earth did this mess come from?"

"It just walked in the door, Ruth," Gram said. "Kelly and I both tried to stop it, but it pushed its way on past us and . . ."

Mom laughed. "Oh, all right. But do you have to do this right in the middle of the kitchen?"

Gram stood up. "Probably not. Come on, Kelly. I'll help you get set up on your desk upstairs."

Mom insisted that we spread newspapers on the floor and sheets of plastic over my desk and bed. "Now try to be careful, Kelly," she said, giving the room one last look, as if she'd never see it in livable condition again.

After she left, Gram closed the door. "The way she acts, you'd think you were going to stand on your bed and sling the paint across the room. I should have had you come out to the farm to do this. We still could. You want to pack up and spend the weekend with us?"

"No, it's okay. Mom won't bug me if I stay in here. She considers this room a lost cause. Besides, if I spend all my time moving around, I won't get anything done."

"You'd probably be better off without me sticking my two cents in every few minutes, too. I'm going to be pretty busy myself, with those windows. Call me if you hit a snag, though." Gram winked and left. I heard a brief exchange between her and Mom in the kitchen, then the sound of the old pickup truck starting up and driving off.

Mom was back upstairs in a flash. "I hope you're not getting involved in some project that's going to take time away from your schoolwork, Kelly. I know how your grandmother gets obsessed with her art work, and I don't want that to happen to you."

"I'm not going off the deep end, Mom. This is just a project for school, that's all." That was almost true. It was a project, and I was taking it to school.

After Mom left, I went back to my painting. I had a hard time at first. This was one job where the old fake-out wouldn't do me any good at all. I purposely didn't look at the pictures in my fairy tale book, even though there were about six of them in *Cinderella*. I wanted these to be my own ideas, not just copies. Each time I got stuck,

I closed my eyes and tried to visualize the way I wanted it to look.

Once, when Gram took me to the Museum of Fine Arts in Boston, she showed me some paintings by a French artist named Monet. There was one that I especially loved. When I stood very close, it looked like little blotches of color. I couldn't even tell what it was supposed to be. Then, as I moved back from the painting, a beautiful cathedral with a tall spire appeared. It was a lavender gray, but it looked as if it had light sparkling through it. That's how I wanted to paint the scenery. It might look weird close up, but from the audience, it would be magic.

In my new version of the castle ballroom, I made a raised platform with the thrones for the royal family and a tall canopy overhead. The drapes falling from the canopy were pulled up at the sides by golden lions' heads. Then I painted a row of banners leading out from each side of the throne and added some balconies. For once, I was going to do something the right way, instead of faking it.

By Monday morning, I had finished paintings of the castle ballroom, Cinderella's cottage, and the village square. I could hardly wait to show them to Mr. Foland.

When I went into my homeroom, Mrs. Isaacs called me over to her desk. "Mr. Foland would like you to stop in his classroom right after last period, Kelly. He didn't say what it was about."

"Oh, thanks, Mrs. Isaacs. I've been expecting to hear from him."

The rest of the day I couldn't think about anything but painting the scenery.

Ladies and gentlemen, we're coming to you today from the Museum of Fine Arts in Boston. This is the opening of a new exhibit of set designs by the incredibly talented Riverton Junior High sixth-grader Kelly MacDonald. As you can see, the gallery is packed with enthusiastic art lovers . . .

I was dying to tell Lisa and Rebecca about my new project, but when I sat down at the lunch table that day, Lisa didn't even look up. Rebecca moved her stuff over to make room for me, though. "Thanks, Rebecca. How's the play going? Have you learned your lines yet?" I hoped she didn't have to remember anything longer than a locker combination.

Rebecca beamed. "Yes, I have everything memorized."

Lisa snorted. "She has two lines in the ballroom scene. 'Yes, Your Highness' and 'No,

Your Highness.' Real Academy Award material."

"Well, that doesn't matter," Rebecca said. "I'm having a great time, anyway. I've met some really nice kids. And you should see the costume I'm going to wear, Kelly. It's beautiful. Rows and rows of ruffles."

Lisa flicked her hair back over her shoulder, a habit I noticed she'd picked up since she'd become a star. "I have *four* costumes. The one for the ball is made out of satin, not cotton like the ones for the chorus."

Rebecca's face got red. "I may not have a lead like you, Lisa, but I'm working just as hard. We have three chorus rehearsals after school this week."

Lisa flicked the other side of her hair. "Well, try having a rehearsal every day after school. That's why they chose only honor students to play the leads. It's really a strain, academically speaking."

I couldn't let that one pass. "You're really a pain," I said "...academically speaking, of course."

Lisa's eyes narrowed. "There are some people who don't have any demands on their time at all, which is a good thing because they are rather limited in the brain and talent departments."

"Are you speaking of anyone in particular?" I

asked. "Or are you just flapping your big mouth as usual?"

Lisa gathered her lunch stuff and got up. "I never realized before how immature you are, Kelly. I can't imagine why I ever bothered with you for a friend." Rebecca and I watched as Lisa stormed across the cafeteria to sit at a table of older kids.

"Don't pay any attention to her, Kelly," Rebecca said. "Those are the kids Lisa hangs around with a lot now. Most of them have leads in the play. That's the fairy godmother, the stepmother, and the king at the end of the table."

"I can't believe the way Lisa's acting," I said. "Is she always like this?"

Rebecca nodded. "She's really been putting me down lately. This star stuff is going to her head. I sure wish you were in the play, too. I never have the nerve to talk back to her like you just did. I really need to have you around."

"Well, I'm going to be around from now on," I said.

"Really? You're in the play?"

"Not quite, but almost." I told Rebecca what Mr. Foland had said about me being the set designer.

She hugged me. "That's great! It'll be just like old times."

"I hope so. But we'll have to do something to get Lisa off her high horse."

"She'll be different with you there, Kelly. You can always make her laugh. She just makes fun of me."

I felt a little twinge of guilt for all the times I'd made fun of Rebecca myself and made a promise to be nicer to her from now on.

After last period, I practically flew to Mr. Foland's classroom. He was sitting at his desk, and the last few kids were leaving as I reached the door. "Kelly, come on in."

"Hi, Mr. Foland. Here they are." I spread out the four paintings on his desk.

Mr. Foland let out a low whistle. "I had no idea. These are wonderful, really wonderful. You must have put a lot of time into this." He picked up the paintings one at a time, studying them closely.

"I can't wait to begin painting the real scenery on stage. How soon can I start?"

Mr. Foland put down the painting he was holding, cleared his throat a couple of times and stroked his beard. "Kelly, we have a bit of a problem here. Mr. Sampson had already chosen a set designer when I spoke to him. It's a ninth-grader, Janet Poole. Do you know her?"

A little voice in my head was saying, *Oh, sure, Mr. Foland. I know all the big shot ninth-graders. I spend every waking moment with every ninth-grader I can get my hands on,* but I didn't say anything. I just shook my head.

"I'm sure you're disappointed, but it doesn't mean you can't work on the sets. I'm going to give your name to Janet so you can be on her crew. She has her own designs, but I'm sure she'll welcome your suggestions."

My inner voice was talking again. *Oh, you bet, Mr. Foland. I mean, if there's one thing I've noticed about ninth-graders, it's how happy they are to welcome suggestions from us sixth-graders.* This time I nodded.

Mr. Foland looked at the paintings again. "It's a shame, really. These are so good. Maybe if you'd come to me sooner . . . well, it will work out for you, Kelly. I know it will. You must have inherited your grandmother's artistic talent."

Yeah, and a whole lot of good that did me. I was back to good old nothing Kelly again. All that work hadn't made any difference at all. "Thanks, Mr. Foland. I'll get these out of your way." I scooped up the paintings and ran out.

The art world was stunned to learn today that the incredibly beautiful set designs by sixth-grader Kelly

MacDonald, recently on display at the Museum of Fine Arts, will not be used in Riverton Junior High's production of Cinderella. *Authorities at the school had the nerve to offer MacDonald a menial job on the set crew under the direction of an obscure ninth-grader. MacDonald turned them down, saying she would be too busy traveling to Paris for the opening of her new exhibit at The Louvre.*

CHAPTER 8

Rebecca was waiting for me in the front hall. "I almost gave up on you. I went up to your home-room, and Mrs. Isaacs said you had to see Mr. Foland. Was it about the sets?"

"Yeah. It was about the sets, all right." I turned away so that she wouldn't notice the tears in my eyes. "I'll see you, Rebecca. I have to get right home."

"But wait. I have to stay for rehearsal. Can I tell Lisa about you being set designer?"

"No!"

"Oh, I get it. You want to tell her yourself so you get to see her face when she finds out that you . . ."

I whirled around to face her. "I didn't get the job, Rebecca. They gave it to some stupid ninth-grader, so forget all that nonsense about things being the way they used to. It's just going to be you and Lisa from now on."

Rebecca looked as if she'd been slapped. "Kelly, I'm really sorry. Do you want me to quit the play so you and I can do something else together? Lisa wouldn't even notice if I wasn't there."

"That's stupid, Rebecca. Why should you quit just because I'm not in it?"

Rebecca stood there cracking her gum for a minute. That was always a sign that she was thinking. "Wait a minute. Won't they even let you help paint the sets? You'd be great at that."

"Well, yeah, that's what I'm supposed to do, but they won't be using my designs."

"So what's the difference if you're not the one in charge? If you're working on sets, we'll still see each other at rehearsals, won't we?"

"Yeah, I guess so." I hadn't thought about that.

Rebecca grinned. "So everything's going to be okay after all."

For a while, I thought it would be.

Thursday morning, an older girl came into homeroom and spoke to Mrs. Isaacs. She looked as if she'd just stepped out of the latest issue of

Teen Scene. Her clothes and makeup were perfect. Even if I copied everything one of those magazine models was wearing, I wouldn't look like that.

Suddenly I realized that Mrs. Isaacs was calling me. I went up to her desk. "Kelly, this is Janet Poole. She wants to talk to you in the hall."

I followed Miss Teen Scene through the door. Three of her friends were waiting for her, another model type and two overgrown males.

Janet's cover-girl smile evaporated as soon as we got out of the room. "Look, kid, Foland said I have to use you on my set painting crew, so here's the schedule." She had a voice like fingernails on a blackboard. "We start next week. Bring grungy clothes to change into because it's going to be a messy job. You'd better be willing to work hard."

Janet didn't seem like the friendliest person I'd ever met, but maybe she'd change her mind if she saw my set designs. "Janet, I have some paintings I did for the four scenes in the play. Would you like to see them?"

The taller of the two boys started to pull Janet away. "You said you just had to drop off a schedule. Wrap it up, will you?"

Janet shook her arm loose. "Wait a minute, we

have a budding artist here. So, Kelly, you think you're pretty good, do you?"

I ignored the sarcasm and forged ahead. "Well, Mr. Foland liked my paintings, and my grandmother says I have real talent. She's a professional artist."

Janet snorted. "Your grandmother! Grandma Moses, I presume. Hey, everybody, this here's the granddaughter of Grandma Moses."

There were a lot of smart remarks from the others, and they all laughed. Then Janet turned to me. "Let's get something straight. All you do is paint in my designs. It's strictly paint-by-number, no creative expression on your part. You still want to do it?"

"Yeah, I'll do it," I mumbled. I was tempted to back out, but this was my last chance to be a part of the play.

As I turned to go into homeroom, I could hear one of the boys say, "Granddaughter Moses!" and they all had another laugh.

I called Gram right after school that night. After meeting Janet Poole, I felt so rotten I needed a little sympathy. "Kelly, I thought I would have heard from you before now," Gram said. "What happened with your set designs?"

"I should have called sooner, Gram. I really worked on the paintings, and Mr. Foland loved them."

"That's wonderful. Tell me more about your sets. When do you start?"

"Well...it's not quite the way I thought it would be."

"Oh? Why not?"

I took a deep breath. "They already had someone else, so I'm not in charge of sets. I'll just be working on the crew, painting somebody else's designs."

"Well, that's too bad, but set painting will be a good experience for you. Maybe next time you'll do the designs."

"Yeah, sure," I mumbled.

"Don't be so discouraged, Kelly. You can't always start at the top, you know. Actually, it's good that things turned out this way. You might have been in over your head, being set designer. You can learn a lot working under someone else."

"But the set designer is a real pill, Gram."

"Just make the best of it. You'll have to work for more than one pill in your lifetime. I can promise you that."

Why couldn't she understand what I was

going through? She knew how much those designs meant to me.

"Kelly? Are you still there?"

"Yeah, Gram. I'm here."

"We must have a bad connection. I just asked if you wanted to come out for dinner tonight. I'll pick you up and we'll swing by the deli and make a whole meal out of the stuff your mother and sister don't approve of. Bring along your designs so I can see them."

"I don't have them, Gram. I left them at school."

"Okay. I'll see them another time. Look, you know those windows I was working on the other day?"

"Yes, what about them?"

"They've been giving me a lot of trouble, and I'm falling behind schedule. I have a tendency to mess up when I rush. Anyway, I sure could use your help. Could you give me a hand tonight?"

I didn't feel like listening to any more lectures about how much I could learn from Janet Poole, so I made up an excuse about having too much homework.

Gram sounded disappointed. "Don't worry about it, Kelly. It's my problem, not yours. Besides, your schoolwork comes first. Keep me posted on your set painting career. I'm sure this experience will be very good for you."

"Right, Gram." Eating liver is good for me, too, but that doesn't mean I do it. So much for getting sympathy.

I brought my paintings home from school, took one last look at them and shoved them into the back corner of my closet. What was the use? Working for Janet Poole was going to be about as much fun as cleaning out the basement after the sump pump conked out. I spent a lot of time holed up in my room that week, just listening to the radio to make the hours go by. Lisa and Rebecca were both too busy to call.

Kelly MacDonald, world-famous sixth-grade artist, has decided to live the rest of her life as a recluse. She has moved to a remote cave in the Himalaya Mountains. The art world mourns the premature loss of this incredible talent. Edward Foland, Drama Club adviser at Riverton Junior High, is just returning from a visit to MacDonald's cave with his Sherpa guides. He looks terribly dejected. Let's see if we can find out what happened.

Mr. Foland, did you have any luck convincing Kelly MacDonald to return to Riverton?

"No. It's a tragedy. A tragedy. If we'd only given her a chance to be the set designer..."

Do you have any explanation why an artist as talented as Kelly was overlooked for your production of Cinderella?

"It was pure stupidity on our part. I can't believe what we put her through. I ... I'm sorry, I just can't talk about it."

When I arrived for the first set-painting session, there were five other people—Janet Poole, the two boys from the hall incident, and two girls I didn't know. They all seemed to know each other, and nobody bothered to talk to me, or even look at me, for that matter. The sets had been constructed—large walls of muslin stretched over wooden frames, called flats. They were anchored to the floor on wooden jacks.

Janet sat on the edge of the stage and called us all over to sit in the front of the auditorium. Her idea of grungy clothes sure was different from mine. She still looked like a fashion plate. I, on the other hand, looked as if I'd chosen my outfit out of Mom's Salvation Army bag, which is exactly what I had done.

Janet got everyone's attention. "Okay, guys. We have to get moving on these sets. There are four of them, and we only have a month to finish. The set on stage is for act one, Cinderella's cottage."

Janet pulled out a large poster-board painting of the cottage interior. I leaned forward to see it better. It was all right but nothing special. My painting had a lot more interesting details in it, but I wasn't about to push my ideas on Janet again.

Janet pulled out a detailed sketch of each flat. "Some of you will be transferring my designs to the flats. That will be Maureen, Sandy, and Jack. Roger, I want you to mix up the paint to match these color samples. Does that take care of everybody?"

I raised my hand. Janet looked up and saw me. "Oh, I forgot about you, Kathy."

"It's Kelly, Kelly MacDonald," I said.

"I thought it was Kelly Moses," one of the boys said. Everybody laughed. Obviously they'd all heard the story about my first meeting with Janet Poole. I wanted the floor to open up and swallow me.

Just then, the next best thing happened. The back door to the auditorium opened and clattered shut as someone tried to sneak in late without being noticed. It took the attention away from me.

Janet looked up. "I hope you're not going to make a habit of being late. If you are, you can drop out right now."

I turned around just in time to see Michael Granby trying to fold his lanky frame into the seat behind me.

Janet continued. "Let's get started now. Michael and ... uh ... what was it? ... Kelly? ... Just try to stay out of trouble until I find something for you to do."

Everyone got up and started working. Michael climbed over the seat and slid in beside me. "That Janet's a real sweetheart, isn't she? She'd make a great Marine drill sergeant."

"She sure doesn't like me. I think she has a general policy about hating sixth-graders."

Michael grinned. "You noticed. She gave me a hard time when I asked to work on her crew."

"Why do you want to work on the sets? I didn't even know you were interested in art," I said.

"Well, I can't act or sing, so this was about the only thing I could do. Almost everybody I know is in this thing."

"I know what you mean. After I messed up the audition, I thought they were going to let me design the sets, but Janet Poole beat me to it."

Michael stretched one long leg over the seat in front of him. "No kidding? You must be good in art."

I shrugged. "Pretty good."

"I bombed out on the audition, too," Michael said. "My voice is changing, so I never know if it's coming out high or low. I sounded like a duck with laryngitis."

"I thought I was the only one who loused up."

"No way! You should've stuck around. There were a few kids who were worse than the two of us put together."

"That bad, huh?" I relaxed and slid down into my seat. Maybe I was going to make a new friend in this school after all. Who ever thought it would turn out to be Michael Granby?

CHAPTER 9

Dad was in the kitchen when I came downstairs the next morning. "Where's Mom?" I asked.

"She went into the city to shop with a couple of her friends. I'm supposed to tell you that your lunch is on the counter and she expects to be back by the time you get home from school."

"Okay, but I'll be getting home late today," I said without thinking, as I grabbed my lunch.

Dad poured himself a cup of coffee and settled in at the table with his morning paper. "Did you tell your mother? You know how she worries if you're late."

"No. I was going to tell her this morning."

"Better leave a note, then. What are you staying late for, anyway?"

I went over and sat across from him at the table. "If I tell you, will you promise not to tell Mom?"

He lowered the paper so he could see me. "What are you doing that your mother can't know about?"

"I'm doing sets for a play."

Dad chuckled. "Your mother's not going to be too pleased about that."

"I know, but Lisa and Rebecca are both in the play, Dad. It's the big school project this fall, and I want to be part of it. It's not like I'm sneaking off to drink or do drugs or something."

Dad reached over to mess up my hair. "You're right, hon. There's no sense in your being left out of things just because your mother thinks the theater is the root of all evil."

"Then it's okay? You'll tell her for me?"

"Sure. If your mother has any objections, I'll handle them."

I jumped up and hugged him. "Thanks, Dad. You're terrific."

Michael turned out to be a real lifesaver on the set crew. At least I had somebody to talk to. Janet never did find anything for us to do that first day. I think she hoped we'd get bored and leave, but we both hung in there. When we showed up the second day and she realized she was stuck with us, she gave us the dullest assignment. We had to paint a wall in Cinderella's cottage. Just a plain flat wall, for pete's sake.

I was grumbling to Michael as we worked. "This is the pits. Janet lets everyone else paint interesting things. Look at the way Maureen is doing the fireplace. I could make the stone chimney look much more realistic than that. Her stones are all mushy, like a pile of giant marshmallows."

Michael looked at me and grinned. "You have yellow paint on the end of your nose."

I was still sputtering. "That's another thing, Michael. This yellow is a putrid color for the walls. In my design, I used rose with a print on it, like wallpaper. It was warm and cozy, like a real cottage. This looks about as cozy as a supermarket."

There was a rehearsal going on today, so our flats were lined up against the wall in the hall behind the stage. We could hear the actors' voices, but we couldn't see anything that was going on. The chorus was practicing in the music room down the hall, and we heard them loud and clear. Even though I wasn't rehearsing with either Lisa or Rebecca, I felt as if we were all working on the same project.

My wall had a window in it, so I figured I'd at least get to paint it in when I finished with the yellow. I could paint a scene in the window, then give it a glazed effect as if it were being seen through glass. I went over to Janet. "I need some paint to do the window now. I guess I'll need green, blue, and white and maybe a bit of brown."

Janet was sitting cross-legged on the floor, making notes on her sketch of the ballroom. She didn't even bother to look up when she answered. "You're not doing the window. Maureen is. Just go over to that last flat and paint in the yellow wall."

"Please, Janet. I know I could do as well as Maureen. At least let me try it. If you don't like the way I do it, Maureen can paint over it."

Janet looked up. "This isn't creative painting class, you know. We have a job to do here, and I say who does what. I don't have time to experiment with some little brat who thinks she's a genius."

"I never said I was a genius, but I'm as good as you are." The minute the words were out of my mouth, I regretted them.

Janet jumped to her feet, eyes flashing. "That does it. You wouldn't even be here if you hadn't conned Foland into thinking you were so great. If you give me any more flack, you're out. Is that clear?"

You could've heard a mouse breathing on that

stage. All eyes were on me as I picked up the can of yellow paint, went over to the last flat and started painting. The sickly yellow paint looked blurred through my tears. Michael came over and joined me. "Why did you say that to her? You crazy or something?" he whispered.

I bit my lip and stabbed at the flat with my brush.

Ladies and gentlemen, we're coming to you from Riverton Junior High where there has been a terrible accident. Janet Poole, a ninth-grader, has accidentally drowned in a huge vat of yellow paint. The Riverton County Sheriff's Department is on the scene.

Could you tell us how the accident happened, Deputy?

"We're not sure. It's the strangest thing I ever ran into. I do know one thing, though."

What's that?

"The color of that paint alone would be enough to kill a person. That's the most putrid yellow I ever saw."

It took all week to finish the cottage set. Michael and I weren't allowed to do anything but flat background painting, so we had the rest of the week off while the others painted in the fun stuff.

On Monday morning, there was a note for me

in homeroom. It was in Janet's scribbled hand-
writing. "Set painting Tuesday afternoon—
ballroom set."

This would be the test of how Mom felt about
the play. I had avoided the subject ever since I'd
talked to Dad. Tuesday morning after breakfast,
I got up my courage. "Don't forget, I'll be late
getting home tonight, Mom."

Mom looked up from packing my lunch.
"What do you mean, 'don't forget'?"

"Didn't Dad tell you?"

"Apparently not. What's up?"

How could he have forgotten? Now I was in a
real mess. I tried not to show I was upset.

"Oh, it's nothing, Mom."

Mom had started to hand me my lunch, then
pulled it back. "Not detention, I hope. Did you
get in some sort of trouble?"

"No, nothing like that. It's just a . . . a club. Remember? I told you Rebecca, Lisa, and I were
joining one."

"Oh, that's right. You never told me which
one, though."

I could have said it right then. I could have
opened up my mouth and said, "The Drama
Club." But I chickened out, and what I said instead was "The Home Ec Club."

Mom gave me my lunch and a hug. "That's

wonderful, Kelly. Did you know that Robin was president of the Home Economics Club for three years in a row? She used to practice her recipes on us, remember? You can do that, too, any time you want."

"Thanks, Mom, but it may take a while before I'm any good. I wouldn't want to poison you or anything." I flew out the door before I could get in any deeper. I didn't like lying to Mom, but there didn't seem to be any choice. To make matters worse, now she thought I was following in "Super Sister's" footsteps.

Nobody else was in the auditorium when I got there after school. The flats for the ballroom set were on the stage. The design had been sketched in with charcoal, but the flats hadn't been painted yet. Michael showed up a few minutes after me.

"Where is everybody?" I asked.

"The leads are rehearsing in the music room with the chorus, but I think we're supposed to be here."

"It would be just like Janet to have the crew working somewhere else and not tell us," I said. "Let's go out and get some fresh air until somebody shows up."

The large doors at the back of the stage were

open, so we went out and sat waiting on the steps. The hills beyond Riverton were a blaze of color, and the air was getting crisp. I loved fall, but this one was slipping by before I could get to the farm to enjoy it. My climbing tree would be a beautiful gold by now. I'd have to call Gram as soon as I had a chance. Maybe I could spend next weekend at the farm.

"You look like you're doing some deep thinking," Michael said. "What's up?"

"Oh, nothing. I was just enjoying the view."

"I'm surprised you're sticking out this whole set-painting thing, Kelly. Janet sure isn't making it easy for you. Why haven't you quit?"

I shrugged. "Part of it is kind of fun. I like being with you."

Michael's face turned red. He looked away from me and stared hard at his size-twelve sneakers. "Yeah, me too," he mumbled.

"There's one thing I don't understand. Why did you use to tease me so much? I thought you really hated me. I sure hated you."

He retied a shoelace. "I couldn't think of any other way to talk to you. You aren't stupid like a lot of the girls. I didn't know I was really bothering you, though."

"It's okay. I guess your clown act is a lot like

my fake-out act. The only trouble is that neither of them really work."

Michael nodded, and we sat in a comfortable silence until we heard voices coming from the stage. When we went back in, Maureen was helping Janet gather up her sketches. Janet brought her painting of the ballroom over to us.

She ignored me and spoke to Michael. "The rest of us are going to get more lumber. Then we'll start building the flats for the third set in Jack's barn. I want you and your little friend here to paint in the gray areas on the walls. I've drawn in the design on all the flats. Just keep checking with this painting to make sure you're filling in the right places. Roger mixed up enough gray paint in those cans to finish the job."

Jack poked his head through the stage door. "Come on, Janet. My brother's here with the truck, and he wants to get going."

"I'm coming." Janet turned to Michael again. "Try to get all the background painted in before you leave. We'll be back if we finish in time." Then she aimed one parting shot at me. "And you! No creative stuff, understand?"

I nodded. I could hardly wait until the pickup truck drove off. I took Janet's painting from Michael. "This is awful, Michael. Mine was ten times better."

"Look, Janet's in charge, and we have to do her design, not yours."

An idea was forming in the back of my mind. "I'll do her design, all right. But I'm going to do it my way." I knew exactly how I wanted it to look. I pushed the gray paint out of the way and started mixing some pink, light blue, and yellow. I was going to have a chance to do my Monet effect after all, and I couldn't wait to get started.

Michael tried to stop me. "Kelly, don't be crazy. If you mess up Janet's design, she'll kill you."

"I'm going to save her design, not mess it up. When she sees what I've done, she'll be grateful." I picked up a wide brush and started making short choppy strokes of pink on the part of the flat that was supposed to be a gray wall.

"What are you, crazy? Janet's going to have a bird when she sees this."

"Trust me, Michael. I know what I'm doing. Just sit down and keep me company while I work."

Michael shook his head and slumped into the king's throne. "I'll stick by you, Kelly, but we're both going to get murdered."

I kept dipping the brush from one color to

another, wiping it on a rag between colors. I wanted the colors to blend together but not mix completely. I squinted my eyes as I worked, painting in the stones as I went along—not real outlines of stones but just a suggestion of their shape and bumpy surface. In my mind, I could see the painting of the cathedral in the Museum of Fine Arts. I wondered if Monet had felt this terrific when he painted. The colors flew onto the canvas.

Once I glanced over at Michael. He looked miserable. "What do you think so far?" I asked.

"Don't ask. I can't believe you're doing this."

I went back to my work and got lost in the joy of putting the colors together. The next time I turned around to look at Michael, he was asleep. I glanced at my watch. I'd been working for almost two hours. I took a break and went out into the auditorium to check my progress. When I saw the flat I'd just painted, I almost stopped breathing.

It was beautiful, absolutely beautiful. The overall effect was a wall of gray stones, but they were magic stones. The castle wall seemed alive with an energy of its own. I couldn't believe I'd done anything so incredible.

I shook Michael. "Michael, wake up. Look what I've done."

He opened his eyes and stared, bleary-eyed, at the flat covered with splotches of color. "Don't worry, Kelly. I'll paint over it real fast. Janet will never know." He picked up a can of gray paint and headed for my magic wall.

I grabbed his arm. "No, Michael. You have to see it from out here." I pulled him down the steps to the auditorium.

"Let me get this mess painted over before Janet gets back, Kelly. There's not much time left. She's going to . . ." Michael's voice trailed off as he turned and looked at my set. He just stared at it for a minute, then spoke in a whisper. "It's fantastic. How did you do that? It looked so awful up close."

"It's magic. You just have to be a believer. Do you still think we're going to get in trouble?"

"No way! Janet would have to be crazy not to like this."

Just then we heard the pickup truck pull into the parking lot. I ran back up onto the stage so that I could see Janet's reaction when she walked in.

She came through the stage door, with Jack, Roger, and Maureen following close behind. Janet's eyes grew wide when she saw my flat. She just stood there for a minute, staring. Then she turned to us and screamed. "You idiots! Why did

I leave two stupid sixth-graders alone? I should've known you'd screw up."

"Janet, you have to see it from farther away," I said. "Don't go by the way it looks up close."

"You're crazy," Janet shouted. "Get out of here. You're finished on this crew." With that, she grabbed a can of gray paint and a brush and made a wide gray slash across my masterpiece.

I grabbed Janet's arm. "Please, Janet, at least look at it first."

Janet turned to me with such anger on her face, I let go of her arm. "I said, get out of here."

Michael wasn't ready to give up. He stepped between us. "She's right, Janet. You have to see it from out in the auditorium. It's beautiful, honest. Just go look."

Janet smiled at him, an ugly twisted smile. Then she turned and began covering up my painting with a flat layer of gray paint. Michael grabbed my arm and led me to the door.

CHAPTER 10

Michael kicked at every stone in the sidewalk, as he walked me home. "Janet's a jerk. I can't believe she painted over your castle without looking at it."

"Yeah, bummer," I mumbled.

"I mean, if she'd just taken two seconds to go out in the auditorium and look at it, she would've seen how great it was." He kicked a pop can and sent it clattering on ahead of us.

"Sure, and then she would've said, 'Oh Kelly, you're so much more talented than I am. You be the set designer. I'll just be a lowly crew member.' Right?" We caught up with the can, and I slammed it into a telephone pole. "It wouldn't have made any difference if she looked at it or not. I didn't have a chance from the start."

"Yeah, you're right," Michael said. "Bummer."

We walked along in silence for a while.

I started thinking about my magic wall. "You know, Michael, I always knew I was pretty good in art, but I never felt like that before."

"Like what?"

"When I got into that painting, it was like my insides were pouring out."

"Gross!"

"No, really!" I ran a few steps ahead of him and walked backward, facing him. "It was a wonderful feeling, and I can do it again and again. I'll even find ways to get better at painting. Janet Poole can't take *that* away from me."

Michael shook his head. "If you don't turn around, you're going to break your neck." I could tell he didn't have any idea what I was talking about. I knew who would understand, though. Gram.

We'd reached my house. "I'll see you tomorrow, Michael. Thanks for sticking by me. And I'm sorry I got you kicked off the set crew."

"Yeah, I'm really broken up over that. I don't know what I'll do if I can't see Janet Poole anymore." He made a weird face, pretended to stab himself in the chest, and staggered off down the street.

I went inside and called Gram. It would be great to be at the farm again. I let the phone

ring a long time, but there was no answer. I figured she was probably out in the garden with
Gramps. Even if they'd gone to the store, they
should be back by the time I rode out there, so I
left a note for Mom and Dad and took off.

The ride out to the farm was spectacular.
The trees on Wheeler Hill were so brightly colored, it almost hurt my eyes to look at them
in the sunshine. I was so busy looking at the
scenery, I didn't notice that I was almost to
the top of the hill and still on my bike. When
the bike started to wobble, I dug in and kept
cranking. Just before the crest of the hill, I
gave one last push and made it to the driveway.
Maybe this was an omen that my life was going
to start looking up.

As I turned down the driveway, I noticed that
the truck wasn't there. I opened the front door
and called, but the only sound was the hum of
the old refrigerator. I wandered back through
the house, stopping in the kitchen to make myself a peanut butter and jelly sandwich, then
went into the studio.

The window I'd seen Gram working on was
finished and in its frame, and two more from
the same set were next to it. The glass for a
fourth window was on the worktable, but it was
only half finished. I went to take a closer look,

and that's when I felt a crunch under my foot. There were pieces of broken glass all over the floor under the worktable. That wasn't like Gram. She might not be the neatest person in the world, but she never left broken glass lying around for someone to get cut on.

There was a sudden noise in the loft, and I jumped about a mile. I looked up just in time to see Miranda leap from the top of the stairs to one of the ceiling beams. She must have been the culprit.

"Wait till Gram sees that you knocked all that glass off the worktable," I said. "You made a real mess down here." The cat eyed me as she worked her way across the beam like a tightrope walker, her tail swishing the air for balance.

As I was sweeping up the mess, my hand brushed against something hot—the soldering iron. Gram would never leave the iron on unless she was in the room with it. The switch made a loud click as I turned it off, and suddenly the house I'd loved all my life seemed creepy. Something was terribly wrong.

The phone rang, and I grabbed it. It was Mom. "Kelly? Your father found your note, and he's on his way out to get you."

"Mom, something's really weird here. Gram and Gramps aren't here and . . ."

"I know. It's your grandmother. She's in the hospital."

"The hospital! What happened?"

"She had a stroke this morning. Apparently she's been under a lot of pressure to finish up some project. Gramps says she's hardly slept all week, and of course she never did follow a decent diet, even after Robin went to the trouble of planning daily menus for her last year. It's a wonder this hasn't happened sooner."

"Never mind Robin's stupid menus," I cried. "Is Gram going to be all right?"

"We think so. She's resting now. I'm going to talk to the doctor, so I'll know more later. Just be out front when your father gets there, so he doesn't have to look for you."

I locked the front door, pulled it closed behind me and sat on the porch swing. Its rusty chains shrieked at me like a pair of angry birds as I swung back and forth, waiting.

Sixth-grader Kelly MacDonald...screech...was responsible for the events leading to her grandmother's ...screech...stroke today. Kelly failed to respond to her grandmother's recent pleas...screech...for help because she was too busy working on a...screech... stupid play.

CHAPTER 11

"We're going to visit your grandmother tonight," Mom said, as she arranged some of the flowers from her garden in a glass vase. "Aren't you coming with us? She's been in the hospital for three days, and you haven't seen her."

Why would Gram want to see me? If I'd helped her when she asked me to, she wouldn't have had the stroke in the first place. I couldn't face her. "I can't, Mom. Just tell her I hope she's feeling better."

"A visit from you would make her feel better, Kelly. She's asked for you every day."

"Hospitals give me the creeps, Mom. I'll just wait until she's back at the farm. She's coming home soon, isn't she?"

Mom swept the cuttings from the flowers into the wastebasket. "Yes, the doctor said she'll be released on Saturday if she keeps improving.

She's not going to the farm, though. She'll be staying here with us."

"But why here?" I asked. "Gram loves the farm. She'll be miserable, cooped up in town."

"Your grandmother isn't the same person she was before," Mom said, scrubbing a kitchen counter that was already spotless.

"But you said she just had a mild stroke. You said she was going to be all right."

"I can see that she's unsteady when she walks, Kelly, and she's lost the strength in her left hand. She'll be much better off here, with me taking care of her. Besides, she has to go twice a week for physical therapy sessions, and I'll have to take her."

"What about Gramps? Will he live here, too?"

Mom squeezed out her sponge in the sink and attacked the kitchen table. "Of course. They can have Robin's room. It's on the first floor, so they won't have to go up and down stairs the way they do at the farm."

"But where are we going to set up Gram's worktable? And then there's the glass grinder..."

Mom stopped scrubbing and looked at me. "Kelly, you're missing the point. Your grandmother isn't going to be doing any more stained-glass work. She'll have to retire and act her age from now on."

"She can't, Mom. Gram loves doing her stained glass. She wouldn't know what to do without it."

"She'll have to learn that there's more to life than her art projects. It's about time she started noticing something else...like the people who care about her." As Mom threw the sponge into the sink and left the room, I thought I saw tears in her eyes.

I tried to picture Gram acting like a normal old lady, but I couldn't. I wasn't sure what Mom meant about Gram not being the same person anymore, either. How had she changed? My imagination was going wild by the time Mom brought her home Saturday afternoon.

I could hear them arguing before they even got in the house.

"Leave me alone, Ruth. If I can't manage to get out of this blasted car by myself, I'm going to sit here in this driveway until I croak."

"Mother, please. If you'll just let me... Mother, be careful!"

"For heaven's sake, Ruth, quiet down. You'll bring all the neighbors running."

"But wait. You're going to fall if you don't..."

There was a lot of banging around at the side
door, then Gram lurched into the kitchen, making a lunge for the door handle of the refrigerator. She was wearing a matching, bright yellow
pants and top outfit. I'd never seen her wear
anything that went together in my whole life.

Her face brightened when she saw me, although I noticed her mouth seemed to droop
slightly on one side when she smiled. "Kelly, I've
missed you." She let go of the refrigerator and
grabbed me.

I hugged her, feeling her lose her balance
slightly. "I've missed you too, Gram. You look
great."

"Great, nothing," she whispered into my ear.
"Ruth ditched my most comfortable pair of bro-
ken-in jeans and bought this getup for me. I feel
like a walking banana."

Mom came in carrying a metal cane with four
short legs at the bottom and held it out to Gram.
"The doctor said you're to use this all the time
when you're on your feet, Mother."

Gram waved her away. "I have no intention of
hobbling around with that foolish contraption.
Norm can use it for a TV antenna, for all I
care."

Mom hovered around Gram until she got her
settled into Dad's recliner in the living room.

"We can't stay long," Gram said. "I have to get home and finish up that last window."

"Just relax for now," Mom said, poking a pillow behind Gram's shoulders. "We'll talk about the window tomorrow."

Gram's eyes flashed. "I'm not going to be here tomorrow, Ruth, so if you want to talk about it, you'll have to come out to the farm."

Mom cleared her throat. "We thought it would be a good idea if you stayed with us for a bit."

Gram's eyes narrowed. "Oh? Just how long is a bit?"

Mom nervously poked at the pillow to fluff it up. "Only until you're ready to go home and take care of yourself, Mother."

Gram hitched forward in the chair. "Well, good. The bit is over." She motioned to Gramps, who had been waiting patiently by the door. "Come on, George. Let's go home."

Gramps fished around in his back pocket and handed her his comb.

"No, home!" Gram pointed to the door. "For heaven's sake, George, I want to go home."

I could tell a battle was brewing, so I ducked upstairs to my room. Mom must have won, because when I came back a little while later, Dad took Gramps out to the farm to move some of their clothes and stuff back to our house. That

night, for the first time in my life, I thought
Gram looked old.

It was a long weekend. By Sunday night, nobody was speaking to anybody. After supper, I
found Gram sitting alone in Robin's room, looking out the window toward Wheeler Hill. I could
tell she'd been crying.

"Are you okay?" I asked.

She tried to smile. "I've been better. I thought
your mother and I were as different as sugar
and salt, but I've discovered she's every bit as
stubborn as I am."

"I could have told you that," I said, sitting
down on the edge of the bed.

Gram shook her head. "I have to get back
home, Kelly. I know your mother means well,
but I just can't sit around all day and do nothing."

"Maybe you can go home in a few days. If you
humor Mom and pretend you're doing what she
wants, she'll probably get off your case. It
usually works with me."

Gram smiled. "You know your mother better
than I do, I guess. We've locked horns since she
was a toddler. She was always such a demanding
child. Always wanting my attention."

I tried to picture Mom as a little kid, but I
couldn't. If she'd ever been a kid, she'd re-

member what it felt like to be one and not have a fit every time I wanted to do something messy, like painting. "I just thought of something you could do to kill time, Gram. I still have those paints you gave me. You want to use them?"

"I suppose I could." She rubbed her left arm. "Maybe it would take my mind off things."

"Hang on. I'll go get them." While I was digging through the junk in my closet, I found my set designs. I tucked them under my arm, grabbed the paints, brushes, and a pad of heavy paper and went back downstairs.

"I have something to show you." I handed her the paintings.

"Your set designs! These are terrific, Kelly. It's too bad they didn't use them. How are things going on the set crew?"

I sat down on the bed across from her. "I'm not on the crew anymore, but you were right about me learning something from it." I told her about Janet Poole and how I got kicked off the set crew because of my magic wall. "But you should have seen it, Gram. It was really beautiful. And I had so much fun doing it, I could have gone on painting for hours."

Gram's face lit up. "Now you know why I lose track of the time when I work on a window. I love to see it grow and change, and I know what it's going to feel like at the end, when I hold it up to the light and see those colors pouring through. You can't explain that feeling to any-body but an artist." Her smile faded as she awk-wardly opened and closed the fingers of her left hand. "I just hope I'm still going to be able to work on my glass. I don't know what I'll do if I can't."

Suddenly the guilt of what I'd done came back to me and formed a hard lump in the back of my throat. "Gram, I have to tell you something. Remember when you called and wanted me to come out to the farm and help you a couple of weeks ago?"

"When you had all the homework?"

I nodded. "I had some, but I could have come anyway, for a while. I just didn't want to hear any more about how great it would be to work for Janet Poole, so I used homework as an ex-cuse. Then I got so busy after that, I never even called to see how you were doing."

"You have your own life, Kelly. I can't expect you to be coming out to the farm as much as you did when you were younger."

"But I should have helped you when you needed me," I said, choking back tears. "Look what I've done to you."

"Now listen here, young lady..." Gram

grabbed the bedpost and pulled herself over next to me. She put her good arm around my shoulder and rested her cheek against mine. "Don't you believe for a minute that you did this to me. I did it to myself. You got that straight?"

"But if I'd come out..."

"I could have used your help, sure, but it wouldn't have bailed me out. I bit off way more than I could chew this time. I'm just not as fast as I used to be. Your mother's probably right. I should slow down."

"You can't give up your glass, Gram."

"Who said anything about giving it up? I said I should slow down, not grind to a halt." When I looked up at her, the old sparkle was back in Gram's eyes.

Rebecca caught up to me as I was walking home from school on Monday. She'd heard about Gram being in the hospital. When I told her about Gram and Gramps moving in with us, her eyes got wide. "They won't be selling the farm, will they?" Lisa and Rebecca used to go there with me every summer, and they both loved it.

"Not if Gram has anything to say about it, they won't. It's all a big mess right now."

"I hope your grandmother is going to be okay. I wondered where you were this week. I didn't see you working with the set-painting crew."

I'd forgotten that I hadn't talked to Rebecca since the big explosion with Janet. "You didn't hear the news? I got kicked off the crew for being too creative."

"Oh, Kelly, you didn't."

"It was bound to happen sooner or later. Janet Poole and I were headed for a battle from the first minute we met. Besides, it doesn't matter anymore."

"Of course it matters," Rebecca whined. "We'll never see you now."

"Look, Rebecca, I was never even in the same room with you and Lisa at rehearsals, so I hardly ever got to talk to you. How is Lisa doing anyway?"

"I haven't talked to her much more than you have. She doesn't have time for a mere member of the chorus."

Sarcasm from Rebecca? This was a switch. "So she's still being a snob?" I asked.

"She's worse than ever. From what I've seen, she isn't making herself too popular with the other leads. She's acting like a brat, upstaging everybody and overplaying her part."

"Sounds like Lisa's really messing things up for herself," I said. "It's too bad, but it serves her right."

"I know. Things have changed since school started. I thought the three of us would be friends forever." Rebecca stopped when we reached my house. "Do you want to come over for a while? I just got the latest issue of *Teen Scene*. There's a whole section on prom dresses. It would be like old times."

"Thanks, Rebecca, but I want to spend some time with Gram. Mom fusses over her all day, and it really drives Gram up the wall."

"Why don't you stop in to see the rehearsal tomorrow after school, then. Bring Michael if you want. The play is going to be pretty good, I think."

"Yeah, maybe I will."

I hadn't really planned to go when I said that, but the more I thought about it, the more curious I got. Lisa had been so rotten to me, I guess I wanted to go see her making a fool of herself. After school I asked Michael if he wanted to stop in and see the rehearsal.

"Are you crazy, Kelly? You want to run into Janet Poole again?"

"She probably won't even be there. The sets must be finished by now. Besides, we can sneak into the back where nobody will see us. Aren't you curious to see how the sets turned out?"

"Not particularly."

We slipped quietly into the dark auditorium and found seats in the last row. The castle ballroom set was on the stage. "Boy, is that tacky-looking," I whispered.

"It's not that bad. It just isn't as good as yours would have been, that's all."

"Michael, it's ugly. I know ugly, when it's staring me in the face."

"Okay, it's ugly. Can we go now?"

"Shh. They're going to start a musical number. Let's watch it before we leave."

Michael slid down in his seat. There were a lot of people milling around on the stage.

Mr. Foland was sitting toward the middle of the auditorium. He spoke in a booming voice that carried all the way to the back where we were. "All right, everybody. Places for act two, scene one. Chorus, this is the first time we've tried this with the dancers, so leave room for them. Miss Goodrupp, we'll take it from the top."

Miss Goodrupp was at the piano in the orchestra pit. At least you couldn't see her bouncing around too much down there. She played the introduction, and the chorus began to sing. I spotted Rebecca right away. She was smiling and acting out the words as she sang. Most of the kids had no expression on their faces at all. They just looked as if they wanted to get out of there, which they probably did.

Mr. Foland was shouting over the music. "Chorus, look alive. Think about the words. This is supposed to be a big event. The prince is giving a royal ball." The group livened up a bit. Then six dancers came out on stage, doing some sort of waltz. They did a turning leap and the girl on the end crashed into some chorus people.

Mr. Foland jumped to his feet and headed for the stage. "Cut! Chorus, give the dancers room. Remember how we blocked this? You're way over your marks."

He jumped up on the stage and drew a chalk line on the floor. "I don't want to see any chorus members stepping over that line. Let's take it again from the top." They repeated that number until the dancers could do it without any midair collisions.

Then they got to the part where the stepmother and stepsisters arrive at the ball. They were supposed to be doing a pantomime, talking together at the side of the stage, but Lisa made a big deal out of it and moved right into the center of the stage. She gestured wildly, getting in the way of the dancers.

Mr. Foland jumped up again. "Lisa, you're overdoing it. Stay over on stage left. This scene belongs to the dancers."

They started again, and this time they went on to the part where the stepmother and her daughters had lines to say. Lisa managed to get in a position where the other two had to turn their backs to the audience in order to look as if they were talking to her. Mr. Foland stopped them again. "Never deliver a line with your back to the audience. Nobody will hear a word you say."

The stepmother spoke up. "Lisa keeps doing that to us, Mr. Foland. She moves back so we have to turn around."

"Lisa," Mr. Foland shouted, "how many times do I have to remind you? Stick to the blocking as we set it up."

Lisa moved back in place and pouted. They ran the scene again, and everything went smoothly until they got to the speaking parts. This time Lisa was in the right place, but she was overacting like crazy.

"Cut!" Mr. Foland yelled. "Tone it down, Lisa. You're overplaying your part to death."

Lisa marched right up to the edge of the stage. "Mr. Foland, I'm playing this part the way I feel it. If the others would put some effort into their characters, it wouldn't look as if I were overacting at all. It's their fault, not mine."

People started whispering in little groups. Mr. Foland strode down the aisle toward the stage, his face like a thundercloud. "That does it. Everybody take a ten-minute break. Lisa, we need to talk."

I strained to hear what Mr. Foland was saying to her, but they were too far away to make it out. Lisa started out angry, but then she began to look as if she might cry. Other cast members were trying to act casual, but you could tell they were trying to hear what was going on. Finally, Lisa picked up her books and left the auditorium, her face bright red.

Mr. Foland jumped up on the stage. "I'm giving the leads the rest of the night off. We'll be running the musical numbers that include both dancers and chorus. Let's start with the first number in act one."

Mr. Foland headed toward the back of the auditorium. I slid down in my seat, but he spotted me. "Kelly, nice to see you again. I was sorry to hear that the set crew didn't work out. I got the impression that Janet wasn't too open to suggestions from you."

"Yeah, that's about it, Mr. Foland."

"That's too bad. I was hoping Janet would be

above all that superior ninth-grade nonsense. You really had some excellent ideas."

"Thanks, Mr. Foland. It's okay."

Mr. Foland looked at Michael and me for a minute. "You know, I was just thinking. There's another job that needs doing on the show. How are you two at climbing ladders?"

Michael shrugged. "Okay, I guess."

Mr. Foland went on. "I need a lighting crew. I'm bringing in a friend from my theater days to design the lighting, and a senior from the high school will be in charge of setting it up and running lights in the show, but we need a couple of crew members to help out. Would you be interested? It would involve one evening to hang and focus the lights and probably two rehearsals before the show."

"I don't know anything about lights, Mr. Foland," I said.

"You don't need to know anything. Jeff Schaefer is the senior I mentioned. He's done lighting on three or four shows. He can show you anything you need to know. Besides, this is the first time we've used a professional to design the lighting. His name is Fletcher Travis. He's been the lighting designer for several off-Broadway shows."

"I guess I could do it." Michael turned to me. "How about you, Kelly?"

"Sure, I'll do it." The only word I had heard was "Broadway."

Kelly MacDonald and Fletcher Travis, the best theatrical lighting team on Broadway, have just added their magic touch to what is sure to become another smash hit. Rumor has it that they've been asked to go to Hollywood to create yet another...

CHAPTER 12

Fletcher Travis blew in and out of Riverton like a fall thunderstorm. He was the best-looking man I'd ever seen, not counting movies and TV. Suddenly, being on the lighting crew was the hottest job in the play. I had finally lucked out.

Gram was thrilled when I told her about my new job. "Lights? What fun. I've done a lot of theater work, but I never explored the possibilities of lights."

"I don't think I'm going to be exploring any possibilities, Gram. Michael and I are just supposed to do what we're told, and this time I think I'll stick to that."

"Whatever," Gram said. "I still want to hear all about it."

"Look, would you mind not saying anything to Mom about this? She gets really bent out of shape if I get involved in anything that's not . . . well, you know, practical."

Gram raised her eyebrows. "Learning how to operate the lights for a theater production sounds pretty practical to me."

"But not to Mom. She just doesn't think the same way we do, Gram, so don't say anything, okay?"

"You shouldn't have to sneak around to do this, Kelly. You're not doing anything wrong."

"Okay, Gram," I sighed. "I'll tell Mom about the lights the first chance I get."

I really meant to tell her, but when the time came, I chickened out again. We were supposed to have a meeting with Mr. Travis and Jeff Schaefer after school on Monday, and I couldn't take a chance on Mom telling me I couldn't go. I told her the Home Ec club was having a special cake baking meeting. She never even questioned my story, which almost made me feel worse. I wasn't cut out for lying.

Jeff was on the stage when Michael and I arrived. He was tall and blond and not bad looking himself. Things were really looking up.

"Mr. Foland says you kids have never worked lights before, but don't worry about it," Jeff said. "It's pretty easy."

Just then Fletcher Travis swept into the room. He was dressed all in black, with a black turtleneck. It made him look like the villain in a play. That turned out to be an appropriate costume.

Mr. Travis looked quickly around the stage. "What do I have to work with? Where is the rest of the lighting equipment stored?"

Jeff spoke up. "We don't have anything stored, Mr. Travis. Everything we have is hanging right there."

We looked up to where Jeff was pointing. There were a lot of pipes suspended from the ceiling. Here and there, big black lantern-type things were clamped to the pipes, and there was one strip of small lights that reached all the way across the stage. There were a few more of the large lights clamped to several pipes hanging in the auditorium.

Mr. Travis dropped his arms to his sides and hung his head. He spoke quietly, through clenched teeth. "You're not telling me that this is all you have."

Jeff shrugged. "Yeah, that's it. What you see is what you get."

Michael laughed but stopped suddenly when Mr. Travis shot him a dirty look.

"I'm glad you find this amusing, young man. I find it rather pathetic. People in economically deprived areas shouldn't try to put on theatrical productions. If you can't do it well, you shouldn't do it at all."

Economically deprived? Riverton? Who did this guy think he was?

The three of us kept our distance while Mr. Travis stormed around the stage, taking notes and making sketches. He kept mumbling to himself. "Pitiful... Where did they find these lights?... Absolute relics... Should be in a museum... Ed Foland is out of his mind... I can't create anything with this junk."

Jeff looked at me and rolled his eyes. I grinned back at him. He was about to whisper something when Mr. Travis interrupted. "There is nothing here to work with. You'll just have to bring in extra lights from another school."

I spoke up this time. "There is no other school. They only allow one school for each economically deprived area."

Mr. Travis glared at me. "We have a young comedienne in our midst." He turned away with a gesture that made me imagine he was wearing a long flowing cape.

Jeff and Michael were trying to keep serious expressions on their faces, without too much success. Mr. Travis continued: "You'll just have to get more equipment from somewhere. What you have here wouldn't illuminate a midnight scene on a moonless night. I'll leave my design plan and lighting cues with Ed Foland before I depart tomorrow night. You *will* know how to proceed from there, won't you?" He was looking at Jeff.

Jeff scratched behind his ear. "Well...yeah. I guess we can handle it."

With that, Fletcher Travis stormed out of the auditorium. As soon as he was gone, we all sat down on the stage and had a good laugh.

We weren't laughing Wednesday after school, though, when we went to set up the lights. Jeff had the lighting design sheet spread out on the stage floor. It looked like the directions for building a computer.

"That Travis guy really messed us up," Jeff said. "I can't make any sense out of this thing at all. He has lights on here that I never even heard of. And look at the lighting cues." He handed me a thick pack of papers.

I thumbed through the pages, long lists of numbers. "What does all this stuff mean, Jeff? Do you understand it?"

"Well, I know what lighting cues are, but I've never seen anything this complicated. Each one of these numbers stands for a different combination of lights. Usually we just have one or two changes for each scene. The lights are wired so groups of them go on together with one switch. Here, I'll show you."

He took us into the wings to a large plate of light switches on the wall. When he threw the first switch, three of the big lights went on. Then he turned on the next switch and got two more lights.

"Here's another thing. These directions call for each lighting cue to fade into the next one. We can't do it with our equipment, and he knows it. He did this to put us down."

Just then, Mr. Foland came in. "How's it going, Jeff? I didn't have a chance to look at the lighting design and cues. Can you get things set up tonight?"

"Not a chance, Mr. Foland. There's no way we can do this with what we have. Here, take a look."

Mr. Foland looked through the papers, shaking his head. "I should have seen this coming. I thought Fletch would have had the good sense to work around our limitations, but obviously he was trying to make a point."

"What do you mean, Mr. Foland?" I asked.

"Fletch and I went to college together, and he's never understood why I passed up an acting career to go into teaching. He's been trying for

years to persuade me to move to New York." Mr.
Foland handed the papers back to Jeff. "Is any
of this usable?"

"We could set it up with the lights we have,"
Jeff said. "I'll try to change the plan to spread
them around."

"Good. Give that a shot, and see what it looks
like. Then we'll go from there."

Jeff started marking the diagram with a red
pencil. After about ten minutes, more than two-
thirds of the lights were crossed out.

"Let's get going," he said. "This and tomorrow
are the only nights all week that they're not rehearsing. You can't hang lights with people running around under the ladders."

Two giant stepladders were set up in the auditorium, straddling rows of seats, and there was
another on the stage. Going up the ladder the
first time was pretty much like tree climbing. It
jiggled with each step and seemed to sway as I
got closer to the top. I didn't mind it, but Michael looked a little green.

Jeff showed us how to loosen the clamps on
the lights and slide them to another spot on the
pipe. Each light also had a clamp to aim it in a
certain direction. Jeff placed chairs on the stage
where the main action would take place to show
us where to aim the lights.

Then he showed us how to put in the gel, the thin, colored plastic that changed the color of the light. It had to be cut to fit a metal frame in front of the light. Finally, he took us to the lighting booth, and showed us how to focus and run the spotlight.

It was hard work but fun. Jeff was completely different from Janet Poole. He didn't look down on us because we were sixth-graders. After we'd been working awhile, he said, "You guys deserve a break. I'll take you to get some dinner. We can come back and finish up afterward. The custodian will let us in."

I looked at my watch. Six thirty! Mom would have a fit if I was any later. "I have to call home first," I said. I ran out to the pay phone in the hall.

Mom answered right away. "Kelly, I've been waiting dinner. You're much later than usual."

"Well, my cake didn't come out right, so I stayed to do it again. A couple of the other kids have, too. The teacher is letting us cook and eat dinner here, so don't wait for me."

"All this interest in cooking is wonderful, but how are you going to get your homework done?"

"I hardly have any, Mom. I did most of it in study hall."

"All right. Well, good luck with your cake. It's important to learn how to get a light, fluffy texture."

"Yeah, that's what I'm shooting for, Mom. A light, fluffy texture."

I'd be glad when this play was over so that I could stop all the lying. I'd still have to practice cooking at Gram's to cover for the fake Home Ec Club meetings. Sooner or later, Mom would put me to the test. The only problem was, Gram couldn't cook any better than I could. She always had to get "creative" and mess up the recipe.

Jeff and Michael were waiting for me at the door to the parking lot. We all piled into Jeff's car and headed for the diner on the edge of town. We had burgers and Cokes and shared a big order of fries. Jeff was fun to be with. A couple of girls from my homeroom came into the diner. I could tell they were impressed to see Michael and me sitting with a senior. People made such a big deal about what year you were in at school. What difference did it make?

When it was time to leave, Jeff wouldn't let us pay for our food. "This is on me. I get paid to do this, so you should get something, too."

The rest of the time went by fast. Jeff changed some of the connections so that different groups of lights would come on together. He had me pull the switches while he did a final check on the lights.

"Okay, that about does it," Jeff said. "There's no rehearsal tomorrow, so I'll meet you guys here right after school and show you how to run cues. The big tech rehearsal will be Friday noon."

"At noon on a school day?" I asked.

"It's Columbus Day," Jeff said. "We have it off."

I'd forgotten about Columbus Day because the official holiday marked on the calendar was Monday. A few years back, the Riverton Town Board had voted to celebrate all of the holidays on their actual date, instead of having them on Mondays to make long weekends. Except for the post office, Riverton did pretty much what it pleased, no matter what the rest of the country was doing.

Jeff had turned off all the lights except one bare bulb hanging high above the stage. "Okay, let's call it a night," he said. "I'll give you two a lift home."

CHAPTER 13

The phone woke me early Friday morning. It was Mr. Foland. "I'm afraid we have a problem, Kelly. There's been a death in Jeff Schaefer's family, and they're leaving for Pennsylvania this morning. I've done some calling around, but I can't find anyone to take his place. Could you and Michael run the lights alone for the tech rehearsal today and the performance tomorrow? Jeff said you two caught on real fast, and he thinks you can handle it."

He paused and waited for me to say something. Jeff had shown us how to run the lights yesterday, but I wasn't sure we could remember everything well enough to do it by ourselves.

"I don't know. I'll have to ask Michael," I said, stalling for time.

"I already asked him, and he said he'd do it if you would."

I was trapped. "Okay, Mr. Foland. I'll try."

"Good girl. I knew I could count on you. I'll see you at noon."

When I went down to the kitchen, Mom had the air popper going and was pulling a tray of cookies out of the oven.

"Popcorn and cookies?" I asked. "What's this, a special holiday breakfast?"

Mom blocked my hand with the spatula as I tried to snitch one of the hot cookies. "These are for Robin. We're taking your grandparents up to visit her at college today. The fall foliage should be beautiful. We're almost ready, so grab some breakfast and get dressed."

"I just tried to grab some breakfast, and someone almost cut my hand off."

Mom smiled and put two hot cookies on a plate for me. "All right, but have some cereal and fruit, too. By the way, what was the phone call about?"

"It was . . . well, it's the reason I can't go along with you today. There's something I have to do here."

Mom dumped the popcorn into a big plastic bag and tied it with a red bow. "What's more important than going to cheer up your sister? Family comes first, you know."

"Why does Robin need cheering up?" I asked,

grabbing a few pieces of popcorn that had missed the bag.

"She's been away for six whole weeks. She must be terribly homesick by now."

"Yeah, so homesick she hasn't had time to write," I mumbled. If I knew Robin, she was having the time of her life.

Mom either ignored my remark or didn't hear it. "Hurry up and get ready. Everyone else has eaten." She was arranging the cookies in a flat box, alternating cookie layers with waxed paper.

I took a deep breath. "Look, you might as well know. I have to stay home because of the play rehearsal."

Mom looked up. "Nonsense. What does the play rehearsal have to do with you?"

"I'm working on the lights for the show. They needed help, and I said I'd do it."

Mom went back to her layering. "I'm sure they can find someone else, Kelly."

"No, they can't. We're already short one person." I told her about setting up the lights with Jeff and Michael. "And now Jeff has to be out of town and ..."

"You mean this is what you were doing Wednesday night when you told me you were baking cakes? You lied to me?"

"I had to Mom. I knew if I asked you, you'd say no."

"Of course I'd say no. I don't want you getting involved in any kind of a theater production." Mom was slinging the cookies into the box so hard, Robin was going to get a bunch of crumbs.

"It's just a school play, Mom. How is that going to hurt me?"

Gram appeared in the doorway. "It's not going to hurt her, Ruth. Let her be involved in the play with her friends."

Mom slammed the cover on the box with enough force to pulverize any of the cookies that had managed to stay in one piece. "Of course you'll take Kelly's side, won't you, Mother? It's bad enough that you've drawn her into painting and the stained glass, but now the theater."

"Look," I said. "I haven't made a big career choice to run off to Broadway here. This is just a school play."

Gram steadied herself by hanging onto the door frame. "Let her go, Ruth. Don't force your prejudices on her."

Mom and Gram glared at each other. They reminded me of the roosters at Gram's that always picked fights with each other. It wouldn't have surprised me to see feathers rise up in hackles around Mom's and Gram's necks.

Mom turned to me suddenly. "Are you coming with us or not?"

"I told you," I said quietly, "I can't."

"Count me out, too," Gram said. "I'm not in much of a sightseeing mood."

"Fine," Mom said, as she picked up Robin's care packages. "If I weren't so angry, I wouldn't consider leaving either one of you alone. But right now, I don't give a hoot what happens to either of you."

"We won't be alone," I said. "We'll be together."

"That's even worse," Mom said and stormed out of the room. She had Gramps and Dad herded into the car and out of the driveway in two minutes flat.

Gram brightened up as soon as they left. "Free at last." She went to the kitchen phone and dialed a number. "Of all the times for them not to be home," she muttered, dialing another number. After a few minutes, she hung up. "Have they evacuated the whole town and not told us?"

"Maybe everybody's gone to see the Columbus Day parade. It starts pretty soon. Try calling later."

"Later may be too late. I've got to get out of

here before your mother gets back. I hoped one of my friends could take me home."

"You're going to leave while they're at Robin's? Just leave without telling anybody?"

Gram put her hands on my shoulders. "You're the only kindred spirit I have in this family. I need to be free to muddle with my work as well as I'm able. You know I can't do that here, and I can't convince Ruth that I'm capable of being on my own. Besides, now you're getting drawn into the middle of our disagreements. The longer I stay here, the worse it's going to get."

"But why do you need someone to drive you out there? The truck is in the driveway. I'll ride out with you, if you don't want to go alone."

Gram shook her head. "I don't dare try it. Whatever this stroke did, I don't seem to be able to judge space as well as I used to. I bump into things a lot now, and I can't take the chance of doing that in the truck."

"Couldn't Gramps take you when they get back? He'd understand how you feel."

Gram snorted. "George? He hasn't been behind the wheel in almost ten years. He'd be worse than me." She slumped down in a chair. "I feel like a hostage. If I could just get back on my own turf, nobody could make me leave."

"I wish you could ride a bike, Gram. It really

isn't that bad a ride and . . . that's it!"

"Kelly, I never did learn how to ride a bicycle, and I don't think this is the time to start."

"You won't have to. I have an old wagon in the garage. I'll fasten it behind my bike, and you can ride in it."

Gram laughed. "Wouldn't we be a sight! But you're forgetting about the hill. You'd never be able to pull me up that incline by yourself."

"Maybe not, but I'll bet I could do it with someone else." I went to the phone, dialed Michael's number and held my breath until he answered.

"Hello?"

"Michael, it's Kelly. I have a big favor to ask of you."

It took a few minutes to convince Michael I wasn't kidding, but he finally agreed to come right over. He fastened the wagon to the seat posts of both of our bikes with a heavy rope.

"Are you sure this will hold?" I asked.

Michael grinned. "I wasn't a Boy Scout all my life for nothing. You could haul an elephant with this. I can't believe your grandmother's really going to ride in the wagon, though."

"You haven't met her," I said. "She's not your basic grandmother."

Just then, Gram came out. "Look what I

found in your mother's Salvation Army bag, Kelly," Gram said with a big smile. She was wearing her "Save Water, Shower Together" T-shirt and her faded jeans with holes in the knees. "Your mother throws things out just as they're getting good." She shaded her eyes. "The sun's pretty bright. I wonder if your father still has that old garden hat in the garage. Ruth probably threw that out too."

She disappeared into the garage and came out wearing a beat-up wide brimmed straw hat. I noticed that she was walking much better today, with only a trace of a limp.

"Gram, this is Michael."

She held out her hand to him. "I've heard a lot about you, Michael. Thanks for helping us out."

"That's okay," Michael said, shaking her hand. "I hope you'll be all right in the wagon. We'll go slow."

"I'll be just fine, and you go as fast as you want. I used to be fearless on the rides at the county fair." Gram climbed into the wagon and we started off down the street. It was a little tricky at first, because we were kind of wobbly and our bikes almost bumped into each other a few times. Then we started riding farther apart, and we could pick up some speed. Everything

was going fine until we came to the corner of
Cramer Avenue, where there was a whole crowd
of people.

"The Columbus Day parade," I said. "I forgot
all about it."

Michael and I both came to a stop, but Gram
didn't have any brakes on the wagon. "Gang-
way!" she yelled, as she sailed right through between the two bikes. She had dragged us about
ten feet past the intersection before we could
stop her.

A man with a clipboard came running over to
us. "Wait, I have to sign you in." He glanced at
Gram's T-shirt. "You must be the environmental
conservation entry. You can slip right in here,
behind the Sons of Sicily Band."

He handed Gram a little Italian flag and gave
me a shove. Before I knew what was happening, we were a float in the Columbus Day parade.

Gram got right into the spirit of things. By the
end of the first block, she was singing "That's
Amore" with the band, waving her flag in time
to the music. I think she was almost disappointed when we turned off at River Road near
the edge of town and the parade went on to the
town park without us.

"Your grandmother is really something," Michael said as we started up Wheeler Hill. Gram was still singing "Funniculi, Funnicula" in the wagon.

We were about halfway up the hill, cranking away like crazy, when I just couldn't push anymore. My bike started wobbling around, and I almost crashed into Michael.

"We'll have to try something else from here," Michael said. He asked me to hold his bike, while he put a big rock under a back wheel of the wagon to keep it from rolling downhill. Then he untied the bikes and hid them behind a bush, and we started pulling the wagon together.

"This is too hard for you kids," Gram said. "I'll get out and walk."

"We're fine, honest," Michael said. "Just enjoy the scenery."

When we finally pulled up to the house, Gram was so excited she practically jumped out of the wagon. "Home at last," she said, taking a deep breath of the cool air under the maple trees. "I can't thank you two enough."

Gram seemed like her old self now that she was back home. She even made lunch for us—a stick of pepperoni, a jar of kosher dills, and a package of marshmallows. For Gram, that was a three-course meal.

She waved from the porch as we left. Gram was back where she belonged, if Mom would just let her stay there.

CHAPTER 14

By the time we got our bikes and rode back into town, Michael and I were the last people to arrive at the rehearsal. Rebecca ran up the aisle to meet me. She looked beautiful in her costume, an old-fashioned dress with rows of pink and lavender ruffles on the skirt.

"Isn't this exciting, Kelly? I'm so glad you'll be working on the show."

"Yeah, me too," I said, not sure if I meant it or not. All the excitement with Gram had made me forget about the job we had to do. When I tried to remember what Jeff had shown us, my mind went blank.

Mr. Foland stepped up to the center-stage microphone and called for attention. "Listen up, kids. The main purpose of the technical rehearsal is to make sure the stage crew can run the lighting cues, the curtain cues, and the set changes. We'll be doing a lot of stopping and starting, so please try to be patient and pay attention. The head of the lighting crew, Jeff Schaefer, had a family emergency last night, so Kelly MacDonald and Michael Granby are going to be taking over on the lights. I expect you to give them your cooperation."

Lisa was sitting on the edge of the stage. I watched her when my name was mentioned, but her expression never changed.

Mr. Foland went on. "Get ready for act one. We're going to start running it from the top in ten minutes."

Mr. Foland came over to Michael and me with two headsets. "Michael, you'll be in the wings, operating the lighting board the way Jeff showed you yesterday. Only you'll be doing it by yourself, instead of with Kelly."

"Okay, Mr. Foland. I'll try."

"Kelly, I want you to do Jeff's job. You'll be up in the lighting booth, running the follow spot, and you'll read the cues to Michael over the headsets. Here, put this on." He handed me a headset, and clipped the battery pack to my belt.

The headsets had a curved piece with a microphone in it that bent in front of my mouth so I could talk into it without holding it. I took the sheets of lighting cues and headed back through the auditorium. Rebecca saw me and waved.

Sixth-grade lighting expert Kelly MacDonald is on her way to her key position in the lighting booth. She looks cool and professional, wearing her technical communications equipment. Let's follow her as she . . ."

"Bug off," I mumbled to my daydream voice. "I don't have time to listen to you anymore."

The lighting booth had a window that opened into the back of the auditorium. The spotlight, shaped like a big cannon on a stand, filled most of the closet-size room. I switched it on and pivoted it back and forth to get the feel of it. Even though it weighed a ton, it moved easily because it was perfectly balanced. Remembering what Jeff had shown us, I aimed the spot at the front wall of the auditorium, adjusted the size of the beam and focused it so the edges were sharp. So far, so good. As I practiced making the spot swing smoothly across the stage, I caught Michael in the beam of light. He pointed to his headset.

I clicked the switch on my battery pack, and Michael's voice filled my ears. "Testing. Testing. Can you hear me, Kelly?"

"Yeah, fine. I forgot to turn it on."

"Okay, let's run some cues before they start the rehearsal."

"Sure. Hang on." Jeff had redone all the cues, using just the lights that we had. They were written in red pencil in the margin of the script, so I could tell exactly when they should be called.

I took a deep breath and started reading from Jeff's directions. "Ready lights one. Switches two, five, and seven. Go lights one." The entire stage was filled with light for the first musical number. "Ready lights two. Switches five and seven off. Switches three and four on." This one didn't go quite as well. Several groups of lights went on and off.

Michael's voice crackled into my ears. "Hold it, Kelly. This is hard for just one person. Let's do that over."

We ran the act-one cues a few more times until Michael got the hang of it. Even though we were doing everything right, there was something about the whole effect that looked wrong to me.

I could see Mr. Foland take Michael's headset and put it on. "Kelly, are you ready to start?"

I started to feel scared. Somehow, I'd managed to get myself into a pretty important spot. "I guess so, Mr. Foland."

"Good girl. We'll try to run act one straight through, but I'll stop any time you get in a bind. Just have Michael come out from the wings and signal me if I don't catch it. Let's go, Kelly. Kill the house lights."

"Kill what?"

"There's a panel of light switches on the wall to your left that control the overhead lights in the auditorium. Turn them off one by one." I smiled to myself as I clicked off the series of switches. What a feeling of power. Me, Kelly MacDonald, killing the lights!

The music from the overture jangled over my headset. I gave Michael the ready cue for lights one. Then, as the curtain opened, I said, "Go lights one," and the chorus and dancers began the first musical number. The scenery really got to me. It was supposed to be the village square, and Janet had used the same gray as the castle for the outside of the buildings.

I whispered to Michael over the headset. "Janet must have gotten a special deal on gray paint. She sure used enough of it."

"Come on, Kelly. It doesn't look that bad." There was a pause, then I heard him say, "Your wall would have looked really terrific, though."

I wished Gram had seen my magic wall. I was wondering how she was getting along by herself, and I almost missed calling the next cue. Michael's voice brought me back. "Hey, something's supposed to happen here. What's the cue, Kelly?"

I read it off to him quickly and scanned ahead to see what the next change would be. This was no job for a daydreamer. You had to be on your toes every minute. We had to stop quite a few times because of problems backstage with scenery changes.

When we finally got to the last scene, the curtain opened on the castle ballroom. It was dismal. "Michael, you should see the set from out here. Janet Poole could be the interior decorator for a prison."

"You can't do anything about it. Just pay attention to the cue sheets."

"Are you sure you pulled all the switches? You should have three, five, seven, eleven, and twelve."

"They're all on, Kelly. I almost broke my neck trying to flip all the switches at once."

"Well, something's not right. I'm not sure what, but it looks awful."

As I studied the scene below me, I pictured the illustration of the royal ball in my book of fairy tales, with its rosy glow and beautiful lavender shadows. That's when I realized what was wrong.

"Michael, I'm coming down. Don't turn anything off before I get there. I want to look at something."

I ran down to the auditorium and stood on the far corner of the stage, where I could look up and see the lights. The only color gels in the lights were shades of yellow and pale amber. What it needed were some of the deep stained-glass colors that I'd seen in the box of gels when we were working with Jeff.

Mr. Foland was getting up out of his seat. "Good job, everybody. That's a wrap. Be here promptly at six thirty tomorrow night. I want to have plenty of time for warm-up before the opening curtain."

I ran up to him. "Mr. Foland, I know what the problem is."

"Which problem? So many keep cropping up, it's hard to keep track."

"The lighting. It's all wrong. All of the gels are yellow and amber."

Mr. Foland squinted up at the lights. "You're right. I guess Jeff didn't think about the colors when he revised Fletch's plan. Well, we'll have to go with that."

"Could we make a few changes now?" I asked. "We don't have to move any lights, just change the gels."

Mr. Foland glanced at his watch. "We ran overtime, Kelly. Do you really think it's that important?"

"Remember what I was telling you about making magic with the colors, back when I first showed you my sketches?"

"Yes, I certainly do."

"I think I can make that happen with the lights. I'd like the chance to try at least."

Mr. Foland looked over at the set, then nodded. "Okay, you've got it."

As I chose the new colors and wrote them in on the lighting sheet, Michael and Mr. Foland followed the plan, putting in the new gels. It only took a little over an hour, but the change was amazing. The castle ballroom scene was the best. We put deep blue and violet gels on the lights that angled in from stage right, so it looked like moonlight streaming through the high arched windows. I changed the gels from stage left to magenta and deep rose, which gave the whole scene a rosy glow.

Just before we left, Mr. Foland stood back and looked at the deep lavender shadows on Janet's prison gray walls. "You were right, Kelly. It's magic!"

Michael and I were just starting to get into Mr. Foland's car when another car pulled into the parking lot, honking the horn. It was Mom. She slammed on the brakes, jumped out of the car and grabbed my arm.

"Mom, you didn't have to come get me. Mr. Foland was taking me home."

"Just get in the car," Mom said through clenched teeth.

I climbed into the front seat next to Mom and looked back as she started up. Michael was still standing there with one hand on the door of Mr. Foland's car. He disappeared in a cloud of dust as we peeled out of the parking lot.

"That was a *teacher* you just rescued me from," I said. "Not a child molester, for pete's sake."

Mom didn't say anything. She gunned the car down Cramer Avenue and didn't turn when she got to our street.

"Where are we going?"

"Where do you *think* we're going? Just take a wild far-out guess."

In the last-minute excitement over changing the gels and then being practically kidnapped in the parking lot, I'd forgotten about Gram. Now

Mom had turned onto River Road.

"Has something happened to Gram?" I asked.

"Don't play innocent with me. I know you helped her get back out here."

"Gram really wants to be home, Mom."

"I don't care what she wants," Mom said, barreling up Wheeler Hill. "You're going to talk some sense into her and get her to come home with us."

"Me! Why me?"

"Because you're the only one she seems to listen to. She certainly doesn't hear a word *I* say." The car skidded a little in the gravel driveway as Mom slammed on the brakes.

Dad and Gramps were sitting on the porch. The moths fluttering around the light cast spooky shadows on the porch ceiling.

"Where's Mother? Why aren't you watching her?" Mom asked, charging up the steps.

Dad swatted a mosquito. "She seems fine, Ruth. She just wanted to be left alone."

"So you left her unattended? There's no telling what she'll . . . Mother!" Mom had reached the studio ahead of me.

"Land sakes," Gram said. "You're enough to scare a body half to death."

Mom snatched the soldering iron from Gram's

hand. "You can't handle a hot soldering iron anymore. You'll burn this whole house down. Ouch!" Mom slipped the iron back in its holder and sucked on her finger.

"Seems you're the one who can't handle a hot soldering iron, Ruth. I'd put an ice cube on that burn if I were you."

Mom ran for the kitchen, leaving me alone with Gram. "How did your rehearsal go, Kelly?"

"Great! The sets were really gross, but after I changed the colors of the lights, they looked terrific. I'll tell you about the whole thing later, but what about you, Gram? You're not going to let Mom drag you back to our house, are you?"

Mom came back, holding an ice cube to her burned finger. By now, Dad and Grandpa had heard the commotion and had come in from the porch.

Gram ignored them and looked at me. "Not a chance. Look, I can still do it." She handed me the two pieces of glass that she had just soldered together.

I ran my finger over the smooth line of solder. "I knew you could. I'll still come out and help you, though. If I put the copper on the edges of each piece of glass, you should be able to get this last window finished by. . ."

"Kelly!" Mom said. "Don't give your grand-mother false hope about what she'll be able to do."

"But it's not false hope. Gram's going to be okay."

"Not alone, she's not," Mom said, her mouth set in a thin line.

"Your mother's not alone, Ruth," Dad said. "She has your father with her. Besides, she had a very mild stroke."

"Never mind the stroke," Mom said. "My mother has never been good at managing her life. I *have* to take care of her, even though she never took care of me."

"You'll do nothing of the sort," Gram said. She grabbed the edge of the worktable as if she thought Mom was going to drag her away from it. "I'm not budging from here, Ruth, no matter how much ranting and raving you do. I don't need you or anyone else taking care of me."

"Taking care—you don't know the meaning of the words." Mom turned on Gram. "Do you know what it was like having you for a mother? I'd need a clean sweater for school, so I'd go look for the one you'd put in the laundry the week before. You know where I'd find it? In the laundry basket—still dirty! And the meals! Some nights you wouldn't get supper on the table until eight thirty or nine o'clock. You'd have to wake me up so I could eat, and half the time it would just be something like peanut butter sandwiches or cold cereal."

"Ruth, I never claimed to be a great housewife," Gram said, "but our home life wasn't as bad as you make out. You were always comparing us to those perfect American families on TV. I couldn't measure up to that."

"Couldn't measure up? You never even came close! You didn't want to bother with me. All you ever thought about was painting and stained glass . . . and the theater."

"Ruth . . ." Gram got up and came around the worktable. She started to reach out to Mom but let her hand drop when she saw the expression on Mom's face.

"Ah yes, the theater." Mom's eyes were glittering with tears. "That was the clincher, when you ran off to New York to 'develop as an actress' and left your husband and your eight-year-old daughter behind on this farm."

Gram leaned back against the worktable for support. "Ruth, it was so long ago, and I realized my mistake after six months. Are you going to hold that against me for the rest of my life?"

"Do you know how long six months is to an eight-year-old child whose mother has run away?" Mom shouted. "It's forever!"

Mom's words had been loud enough for even Gramps to hear. He went over and put his arm around Gram. "But she came back to us, Ruth," he said quietly. "That's the part you never understood. She came back."

"Sure she came back," Mom said, "and that was almost as humiliating as having her run away in the first place. How was I supposed to explain it to my friends, when I didn't even understand it myself? You were no help, Father. Every time I tried to ask why, you'd just say, 'Now, now, Ruth, the important thing is that she's back home.' I think you were just as scared as I was that she'd leave us again."

"I think we'd better go home now, Ruth," Dad said. "All this shouting isn't going to do anyone any good." He tried to steer Mom out of the room, but Gram held up her hand.

"Let her talk, Norm. This discussion is about thirty years overdue."

Mom started to say something to Gram, then stopped herself when she noticed the piece of soldered glass I was still holding. "I used to love your grandmother's beautiful windows, Kelly," she said, taking the piece of glass from me. "I'd sit in the studio for hours watching her work, just like you. And I was so proud of her when

she had the lead in the PTA play every year. She
was wonderful, and she looked so beautiful on
stage with her long red hair. But she wasn't the
kind of person you could have for a mother—
someone you could really count on. She was
always too wrapped up in her own interests."

"I didn't mean to neglect you, Ruth," Gram
said. "It's just that I'd get caught up in a painting
or a stained-glass window, and the time would
disappear."

Mom turned to Gram. "Do you remember
what time of year you left us, Mother?"

"It was so long ago, I can't..." Gram rubbed
the knuckles of her left hand, then looked up.
"Was it spring? Late March or maybe April?"

Mom's cheeks were wet with tears, but she
didn't bother to wipe them away. "Yes, it was
spring, when every female animal on the farm
was raising a new brood. Every time I saw the
kittens or the chicks or even the baby mallards
on the pond with their mothers, it reminded me
that you were gone." Mom's voice was small now,
almost like a child's. "Mothers and their children
are meant to be together. Even the animals knew
that. Why didn't you? Why didn't you love me?"

Gram was starting to cry as she stood there
facing Mom, but neither of them made a move
toward each other. "I've always loved you, Ruth,

but I'm not good at showing it. Maybe people like me shouldn't try to be mothers."

I couldn't stand to see them both hurting like that, but I didn't know what to say. I stepped between them. "If you hadn't been a mother, Gram, I wouldn't be here at all."

Then a strange thing happened. They both said, "Oh, Kelly," almost at the same time. And they each reached out to hug me, but all of a sudden we were all in this big three-way hug.

"Please don't fight anymore," I said.

Gram answered me, but she was looking at Mom. "This isn't a fight, Kelly. If a bone is fractured and it doesn't set right, sometimes you have to break it again to get it to heal."

CHAPTER 15

Gram and Gramps never did come back with us that night, and Mom barely said a word all the way home. She was still quiet the next morning. Then she went for a long drive in the afternoon, saying she had a lot of thinking to do. She hadn't come back by the time I had to leave.

"Are you and Mom coming to the play?" I asked Dad as he drove me to the school.

"I'll be there, Kelly. And if your mother is feeling better, I'm sure she'll be there, too."

"You mean, if you can talk her into it."

Dad looked over at me and smiled. "Whatever."

"What about Gram and Gramps? Gram's afraid to drive now, so they'll need a ride. Do you think Mom and Gram will ride in the same car together?"

Dad pulled up to the school entrance. "You

155

just go in there and do a good job and let me worry about the travel arrangements. I'll run a shuttle bus, if I have to."

Michael met me backstage. Then I went up into the booth, and we practiced a few of the toughest lighting cues before the audience started to trickle in. I tried to keep my mind on calling the lighting cues, but I couldn't help but think about Mom and Gram. For the first time, I realized how lonely and scared Mom must have been when she was a child.

Michael's voice coming over the headset startled me. "Mr. Foland says we have to knock it off now, because cars are beginning to come in the parking lot."

"Okay. I'll be right down."

As I walked past the classroom being used as the female leads' dressing room, someone called my name. "Kelly, could you come in here for a minute?"

It was Meg Hammond, dressed in her "rags" costume for the first act. I didn't think she even knew my name.

"Hi, Meg," I said. "Do you want me to get something for you?"

"No. I just wanted to say that you and Michael are doing a great job. You're really saving my life in the ballroom scene with that spotlight of yours."

"Really? How?"

"I was terrified of my solo in that scene because it has so many high notes. I had an awful time with it in the early rehearsals. Then, when you started using the spotlight, I was so blinded I couldn't see anyone in the audience. Now I just pretend nobody's out there, and I don't get nervous at all."

"Well, I'm glad it helps," I said.

As I turned to leave, I could see Lisa sitting alone on the other side of the room. She saw me looking and turned away.

I went over to her anyway. After all, she'd been my best friend not too long ago. "Hi, Lisa. Are you all set for the big night?"

She managed a weak smile. "I guess so." She looked down at her lap and bit her lip. Suddenly, the old Lisa was looking up at me, her eyes huge with the heavy eyeliner and mascara. She leaned forward. "Kelly, I'm petrified. I've been sitting here trying to remember my lines. They're all jumbled up in my head. What am I going to do?"

I slid into the desk next to her. "Don't panic. You've rehearsed those lines a hundred times.

They'll come back to you when you get on the stage."

"What if they don't? I'll just die if I go out there and make a fool of myself."

"That's not going to happen. Everybody gets stage fright. Even Meg Hammond." I told her about Meg and the spotlight.

Lisa looked over at Meg. "No kidding? I didn't think anything made her nervous. She's so good."

"So are you. Just remember the old fake-out. Nobody will even guess that you're scared. I'll be rooting for you up in the lighting booth."

"Maybe when the play is over, we could hang out together again," Lisa said. "Rebecca, too. I've missed you guys."

"Sure," I said. "Why not?" Things might not be quite the same between us, but there was no reason we couldn't still be friends. I held out my hand and we did a two-person version of our old secret handshake. Then I went to find Michael.

Backstage was a madhouse, with people moving pieces of scenery around. Michael was in his usual corner by the lighting board. "Where have you been? I thought you got lost."

"Just sidetracked. Are you ready?"

Michael rubbed the palms of his hands on his jeans. "I don't know. If my hands don't stop sweating, I'm going to short-circuit the whole board."

I punched him in the arm. "Come on. We're a great team. Granby and MacDonald will be the toast of Broadway someday."

"Yeah, sure. Listen, Kelly, just stay awake up there, will you? No daydreaming?"

"Okay, I promise. See you later."

It seemed strange to look down from the lighting booth and see so many people in the auditorium. I stuck my head out the window and looked around for familiar faces, or rather familiar tops of heads, but it was hard to recognize people from this angle. I didn't see anybody from my family.

The auditorium was starting to fill up fast. Dozens of conversations drifted up to me, like the humming of a giant beehive. This was better than sitting up in my climbing tree. Members of the orchestra were starting to come in now, adding their tuning-up sounds to the beehive. Still no sign of the family. Dad's shuttle bus plans must have bombed out. Suddenly, I remembered to turn on the headset.

"Michael, I'm here."

"Kelly, you make me crazy. What took you so long?"

"Sorry. You have my undivided attention for the rest of the evening."

"Hang on a minute. Here's Mr. Foland."

There was a rustling sound in my ears as Mr. Foland took the headset. "Kelly, I just thought of something I forgot to mention before. When Mr. Eastway, the orchestra conductor, makes his entrance, pick him up in the spot and keep it on him until he finishes his bow and starts the overture."

"Okay, Mr. Foland."

"How does the house look?"

"What house?"

"The audience. Are the seats filled up?"

This theater business had a language all its own. Every time I thought I knew enough "stage talk" to sound cool, some new phrase would crop up and make me look dumb. "Yeah, Mr. Foland, most of the seats are filled. A lot of people are still coming in, too."

"Great. We'll be starting in about two minutes. I'm giving the headset back to your partner. I'm going to cue Mr. Eastway right now. Flash the house lights three times and take them down slowly. That will get the stragglers into their seats."

I did the house lights and moved the spotlight into position. It was a little tricky, because I had to have the light off when I aimed it. Then, when I flicked the light on, it wasn't always where I thought it was going to be. I could see the side door opening and was all set to flip the switch, when I realized it was only Harvey De-Mott's father trying to sneak in late. He came real close to being very embarrassed.

The door opened again, and this time I caught Mr. Eastway in my spotlight. Right on target! I was getting pretty good at this.

The overture started, giving me goose bumps. I called the lights-one-ready cue. When the curtain opened on the first musical number, the chorus and dancers were posed like statues. The scene was so beautiful it almost took my breath away. The audience must have thought so too, because they applauded before anybody did anything at all.

It was so different doing the show with an audience. They laughed in all the right places and clapped like crazy after every number. Of course, most of the people in the audience were related to somebody on the stage, but it still was a great show.

It all went by too fast. As Cinderella came down the staircase in the ballroom scene, we added one of the pink lights each time she took a step. It looked as if she was drawing the magic into the room with her. Then she started her solo, and I framed her face and shoulders in the spotlight. Meg didn't seem nervous at all. Her hair was pulled up in back and cascaded down in curls. She had a sparkly little crown on her head that caught the light as she moved.

By now, Lisa's stage fright was completely under control. She'd seemed a little scared at the beginning, but she relaxed as the play went along. Now she really got into her comedy song with the other stepsister. The audience liked it so much, the stepsisters had to do an encore right in the middle of the show.

Much too soon, the music started for the finale, and Cinderella's wedding procession began. Meg looked beautiful, her long white veil held with a wreath of flowers. Then, in a blur of color, it was over—the final dance, the curtain calls, and the audience on its feet, cheering. I switched off the spotlight, letting the fan run to cool it off, and watched the people filing out of the auditorium.

Michael's voice sounded excited. "We did it, Kelly. Not a single hitch! Are you coming down?"

"Just let me cool off the spotlight a bit more. I'll meet you at the reception in the gym."

CHAPTER 16

By the time I got downstairs, it looked as if the whole population of Riverton was trying to squeeze into the gym. I spotted Dad towering above the crowd in the far corner and started working my way across the room. At least he had made it to the play.

Before I got to him, I ran into Gram. She reached out and took my hand. "The lighting was wonderful, Kelly. I think all those years of holding stained glass up to the sunlight finally paid off for you."

"Gram! I was afraid you hadn't come. How did you get here?"

"Ruth called to say she and Norm would pick us up."

"You all came together? Does this mean everything's okay between you and Mom now?"

"You can't wipe out thirty years of resentment

in one night, Kelly, but I think we've made a start."

"Oh, I hope so." I hugged Gram, and as I looked over her shoulder, there was Janet Poole with a couple of her friends.

One of them was gushing all over her. "Janet, your scenery was absolutely beautiful, especially the ballroom scene. How did you know to use that beautiful rose color on the walls and those luscious purple shadows?"

Janet was beaming. "It just comes naturally for an artist, I guess."

I couldn't believe it. Janet was going to take credit for my work, after I saved her ugly sets with my lighting. Gram must have felt me stiffen. She whispered in my ear. "Let it go, Kelly. Most people wouldn't understand what you did even if you explained it to them."

"But it's not fair, Gram. I'm not going to let her get away with it."

Gram held me by the shoulders. "When you watched the show from the lighting booth, did you feel proud of what you'd done?"

"Well, sure, but . . ."

"That's about as good as life gets, Kelly. Don't go around needing approval from other people."

I knew Gram was right, but I still had an overpowering urge to punch Janet Poole right in her perfect little nose.

I felt a hand on my shoulder. "I really enjoyed the play, Kelly." It was Mom.

"Kelly did great things with the lighting on this show," Gram said. "She has a marvelous sense of color."

Mom looked puzzled. "Color? But I thought she ran the spotlight."

"That was only part of it, Mom. I got to choose the colors for the gels on all the lights."

"Oh, that's nice, dear."

"Kelly," Gram said. "Take your mother and me backstage, will you?"

"Oh, I don't think we should go back there," Mom said.

"Nobody will mind, Mom. It's this way."

Only the bare white work lights were on as I led them onto the stage. The castle ballroom set was still in place.

"Remember what this looked like during the play, Ruth?" Gram asked.

Mom went over to one of the castle wall flats and touched it gingerly. "It was different... prettier. I don't remember it being this color."

Gram smiled. "The difference is what Kelly did with her lights. I just thought you should see it so you'd understand." She watched as Mom walked around the stage, then winked at me. "You two take your time. If I don't get back to George, he'll think I had another stroke."

Mom looked up at the scenery hanging in the space over our heads. "You really enjoy being a part of all this, don't you?"

I shrugged. "It was fun doing the lights. I want to try designing sets for the next production, though. I think Mr. Foland might give me a chance, now that he knows me. Will that be okay with you? I don't want to go behind your back this time."

Mom shook her head. "You've always been so much like your grandmother. If only I could be sure you weren't heading for the same life that she's had."

Mom walked away from me, then stopped at the prop table in the wings and picked up a glass slipper. It sparkled in the red light of the exit sign, and as she turned it over in her hands, I could see some of the glitter fall off.

She came back into the light from the bare bulb overhead. "Is this what you want? It's all fake, Kelly." Her palm sparkled as she held it out to me. "These may look like glass slippers from the audience, but they're nothing more than an old pair of white shoes covered with glue and cheap silver glitter."

"But Mom, if they were made out of real glass, nobody could wear them."

"None of this is real. Look what you did with your lights." As she gestured toward the set with the slipper, more glitter fell. "You made this castle seem beautiful during the play, but afterward it goes back to being what it always was—an ugly gray muslin stretched on a frame. That's dishonest."

"I'm more dishonest if I pretend to be something I'm not. Maybe you and Robin can walk around in real glass slippers, but Gram can't, and neither can I." I ran up the ballroom staircase so that she wouldn't see that I was trying to hold back tears. Then I turned to face her. "I've finally found something I really love doing—something I'm good at. I'm sorry, Mom, but I just can't be the perfect daughter you want me to be."

Mom looked up at me. "I never said you had to be perfect, but I hate to see you getting involved in all this useless make-believe. Your grandmother has spent her whole life with her head in the clouds. It frightens me when I see so much of her in you."

"But there's a lot of *you* in me, too, Mom. And Gram may be a little weird, but she couldn't change now if she wanted to. Why can't you just

accept her the way she is? And why can't you let
me be who I have to be?"

Mom stood there for a couple of minutes
holding the slipper. When she looked back up at
me, there were tears in her eyes. "I know you're
talented, and maybe I'm a little jealous. I never
could draw or paint or get up in front of anyone
and perform. Sometimes I feel left out, because
you and your grandmother are so close and you
both love the same things."

"Sure we love the same things, which means
we both love you, for starters. And we'd be a
mess without you, Mom. We'd be up to our ears
in paint and stained glass, and you know we'd
never have a decent meal."

Mom laughed and quickly wiped her eyes,
leaving a dusting of sparkles on her cheeks.
"Well, that's the truth. Someone around here
needs to have her feet on the ground. But even
though your grandmother might be set in her
ways, I think you're still young enough to make
a few changes."

"Like what?" I asked, picturing myself turning
into a Robin clone.

"Like keeping your room clean?"

"That's it? I can paint and help Gram with
stained glass and do sets for the next play as
long as my room is clean?"

"Only..." Mom said, "if your schoolwork is done first. And I may think of some other conditions as we go along."

"But what if I turn out to be an artist someday, instead of something sensible like a nutritionist? You won't get all bent out of shape?"

"I'm not promising to like it, but if the shoe fits, Kelly..." Mom smiled and held the slipper out to me. "You might as well wear it."

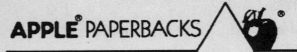